Tales Of Kurla Station

debashis mitra

Tales of Kurla Station

ISBN 978-0-578-96269-6

Powered by Pothi.com

Cover Art by Ashy Dave

Editors:

Debanjan Mitra

Amartya Tashi Mitra

Prasad Boradkar

First read by Shaivi Desai

Being translated to Marathi by Dr Raghunath Boradkar

dedication….

A songbird nudged: "Tell me stories", said she,
"Tales from beyond this sleepy wood,
Tales of the city, its women, men 'n child;
Happy, yet sad, humans: bad, yet good".

And so these tales of my city and its trains:
That recount nothing, not ordinary, nor new,
A myriad collage of acts and deeds,
Played out by people like me and you.

So, to my city do I dedicate these pages
And who helped shape them, plus a memory of few:
Binbin, Ashy, Phutun, Uncle and Prasad,
Mini, Prajakta, Amethyst, Auntie, Ma and my friends
My dear Kaka, Mama,
And you, Baba,….
For every word when I write;

I think of you.

Prologue

The local trains of Mumbai are said to be the 'lifeline of this city', and this little phrase has been oft repeated in many a newspaper and magazine. This little collection of anecdotes revolves around this lifeline and one of the oldest stations to serve it—Kurla Station. I have taken inspiration from my experiences and observations during that time, when I made the journey from my home to Kurla station each day.

The trains, a gift by the much maligned British who were then rulers of India, have crisscrossed the length of this ever growing metropolis since this city was called Bombay. The present rulers renamed the city Mumbai, but none of that mattered to the trains that went about their lives as if nothing had happened. Thick with coats of yellow and brown paint, these trains, like metal worms, have been piercing through habitation, forests, wetland, running over sea, continuing to redefine their domain. A single, original track replicated into many more, each branching off into several venations as the inhabitants of Mumbai moved further and further away until the city started to coalesce with its neighbouring villages, towns and cities, engulfing them all.

Along these tracks, civilizations sprung up. People from all over India, and even the sub-continent, entered the city on these tracks, settled alongside them and built their lives there. These belts of habitation followed a concentric pattern on both sides, starting right from the railway sleepers to the serene bay and the seashore on either side of this bustling spur of land in the Arabian Sea. Eventually, the rich started moving away from the rails to the outer edges of the city, like children moving away from their parents as they grow, the poorer taking their place in the waiting haven as the younger siblings. Even today, there is constant outward flux of people from the core to the periphery, like ripples emanating from this throbbing mother lode. Yet, like children coming back to the arms of the parent, each day people from the outer edges cut across the inner sections and come back, to clamber onto the carriages on steel rails, propelled by wires that carry one and a half thousand volts of electricity. They gather at the stations, those wondrous islands of bustling activity, to use the trains which transport them to their work, their schools, their homes.

But that is not all to these islands. The platforms are not just locations where the mundane chores of getting on and off trains are performed. They are complex microcosms created by humankind, perhaps unlike any other on earth. These concrete stages are buzzing with life playing out its myriad nuances both on and offstage. When one looks down, one finds the seemingly empty tracks teeming with activity: rag pickers poking around with their huge plastic sacks picking up bits of paper, bags and discarded water bottles. Huge rats are out too, foraging for morsels. Add to these: the set of reckless people, who rush to jump down on the tracks, urgently whizzing across multiple tracks to hop on to the neighbouring platforms.

Once one tears one's thoughts away and gazes from the tracks to the platforms, one perceives another world. Everyday routine unfolds in this incessantly regenerating mass of humanity. Every few minutes one looks, there is always the crowd; but faces get replaced. However, within this constant change, there is a permanence. The permanence of the tea stalls selling everything from single cups of tea to mini meals. And the permanence of the poor souls who lead their lives here. The permanence of the beggars, each to his or her position; that never changes, and the permanence of the hawkers, moving around with their ware and goods to sell.

There is a buzzing anticipation as the train approaches the station. Some call out to the mad men on the tracks and haul them up out of harm's way. Soon, a wave of humanity moves across the platform right to its precarious edge, mere inches from the arriving train. Then, before it comes to a complete halt, the masses inside the train tense up in readiness, bodies bulging out of the doors. Some fling themselves out. The throng on the platform steps back in unison, and after an infinitesimally small pause, launches itself at the openings, while the people inside brace themselves for the onslaught. There is an intense, chaotic struggle between competing waves of people trying to get on and off the train. Before one knows it, the train is on its way out and rolls out of the platform stuffed well beyond its capacity and with hundreds just hanging out of the doors, windows and from any handhold that the construction of the train may offer. On the platform, the tide of people recedes, revealing the uncovered patch of concrete for a few brief moments until the cycle starts all over again..

Statistics say that the dreary lives of fifteen people are snuffed out daily, on these tracks. Cést la vie. Fifteen people are hardly missed amongst the multitude that this city holds, and people go about their busy lives paying little or no heed to the casualties or the going ons on these stations.

And a mad life, it is!

But in this madness, one finds humanity playing out its daily game in all its colours. Perhaps there is no singular place where one can perceive every act and behaviour that tends to define us as human beings. There is a story in every corner, on every face.

One has to just look and observe.

That is all that I have done.......

Contents

Popcorn

Thursdays at Kurla station tend to always sport a slightly thinner crowd and this evening was no different.

I had reached the station pretty quickly from the office and was hurrying down the foot-bridge to my platform, only to see a train leisurely leaving, bursting at the seams with home-goers and the usual thick layer of people hanging on the outside. There were still a few desperate people, who tried to bound down the slippery steps to try and latch on to that thick outer coat of humanity. I moved to one side to let the stampeding lot carry on in their urgency to get onto the fleeing train, which accelerated, oblivious to the frenzied punctuality needs of these people. I for one, have never understood what a few minutes would actually mean in the larger scheme of things. The next train would be here in these five minutes and by the time these urgency ridden madmen had reached their destination and then hustled for an onward auto rickshaw ride or bus ride, to their homes; I would probably have narrowed the margin by three minutes. By the time they all, myself included, made it through the traffic, it would be quite possible that we would have evened out completely.

But then, if everyone thought alike, there would be no wars, no strife...so each to his own.

I walked down to the platform to stand next to the book stall, this being my routine and favoured position from where I would fling myself onto the door of the first class compartment that the train would place right in front of me each day. Added to this luxury was the fact that the column next to this place had a large fan mounted on it,

1

which blew a blast of air on me. As my sweaty shirt dried up and heat exchanges took place as per the laws of physics, which did apply to Kurla station as well, I slowly cooled down and was prepared for my leap of faith onto the footboard, to come.

A cursory glance at the announcement board revealed that the next train was delayed by five minutes, and so I found my way to the tea stall a few meters away and asked for some popcorn.

These food stalls make brisk business, selling everything from little packets of biscuits, to fizzy drinks, to curried chickpeas, handed out in overflowing plates along with two buns of local bread. However these stalls are locally called tea stalls, because their major sale is khaki coloured tea that is poured out from the tap of a large, cylindrical stainless steel container. They are typically manned by a manager and several waiters, all dressed in their khaki uniforms and wearing the typical Maharashtrian caps on their heads. Lately, they had added popcorn to their ever expanding menu. For five rupees, the waiter will stuff a small brown paper bag with popcorn, and I found that a great way to pass the time while waiting for my train.

Having procured my goody bag, I started to munch on some kernels ruminatively. Around the same time, a little girl in ragged clothes walked up to the popcorn stall. She must have been about eight and carried the tell-tale woven plastic sack on her shoulder, like all ragpickers did. Her feet were bare and her hair was clipped short in the fashion that necessitated very less care and fewer visits to the barber. I braced myself as she approached and prepared to refuse her, the moment she asked for money. I hate handing out money to beggars and her sorts. But she just walked past me, straight to the counter.

To my surprise, she reached into a little pocket in her dirty pink frock and fished out a five rupee coin and confidently handed it over to the popcorn man. I was tempted to ask the man, not to accept the money and pay for her, but something in her demeanor made me hesitate and in a flash the transaction was done. She disappeared into the crowd with her little brown paper bag of popcorn, dragging her rag-picking sack behind her. It looked empty and I thought she might be returning back home wherever she lived with her earnings, just having disposed of her day's pickings. I mused that she probably would get a scolding from her parents today for squandering a full five rupees on popcorn, something that did not even fill her belly. I kicked myself for my hesitation to buy her some. I comforted myself, thinking that she would probably lie about how much money she had made that day and spare herself from her parent's wrath for her indulgence.

But these situations happen daily on this platform with the thousands that come and go and hundreds who live off it. One gets immune to these little missed opportunities of philanthropy and I too, just dismissed the thought, picked up my change and popcorn and walked back to my spot.

The crowd had thickened by now. A little delay in the almost regular timings of the local trains always meant that the waiting crowd doubled. I decided that if I had to get onto the next train, I should shoulder ahead to the edge of the platform as much as is safe, so that when the train did come, I would be in a better position to make it into the door. That's when I spotted the little girl again!

She was standing right at the edge of the platform and was intently looking over as she munched on some of her popcorn. She ate some and then, to my surprise, threw a few kernels onto the track. I looked back furtively to see if there was a train approaching. She was leaning over and if the train came into the platform, she would surely be hit. There was no train on the horizon and I dared to look more intently. I was intrigued. This impoverished little rag picker had just bought herself a snack, which according to me, she could ill-afford and was now throwing bits of it away!

Her little lips were curved on the edges in a tiny hint of a smile, and in-between shoving popcorn into her mouth, she threw some onto the tracks and leaned over to look. The popcorn fell continually like little white wildflowers in the evening light, onto the dirty grey tracks. I checked back again for the train and dared to lean over to see where they fell. On the edge of the sleepers, sat two grey rats on their haunches looking up at this shower of manna. Their tiny little forelegs, held up like small hands, were holding a popcorn apiece as they looked up at their little benefactor.

There she stood, oblivious to the crowd around her, with little care for the possible danger of the incoming train, taking pleasure in feeding the two rats with a treat that she had bought for herself in her indulgence. My eyes blurred, the crowd faded and I saw the three of them in a glow, helped by the twilight and the joy I sensed somewhere within.

The crowd around me grew restless and the two rats scurried away. I looked up to see the train slowly worming towards the platform. I looked back and she was gone too. I moved back to safety and as I scanned the crowd, I managed to glimpse the dirty white sack and the end of the little pink frock disappearing into the forest of humanity.

The Happiest Man on Platform 7

I don't see this soul anymore... in fact, it has been a year or so and I still look around for him whenever I alight from the train or wait for one in the evenings.

Since the time I began using the lifeline of Mumbai for my daily trudge to work, I had formed a habit of pausing for a bit after being bodily pushed out of the train by my fellow journeymen onto the platform. Retreating to a small uncrowded spot under a fan, I would wait until the stampede to the over bridge subsided, then catching the opportune moment before the next train arrived, I would start on my onward journey over the tracks into Kurla.

One day, a particularly muggy one, I had stopped a little longer to drink a mouthful of water from my water bottle, when I spied a wiry and shaggy man with long hair, filthy clothes and an unkempt beard staring at me with a bemused smile on his face. His eyes and head seemed to follow each movement of mine. Every time I raised the bottle, his face lit up in mirth and he chuckled something to himself. For a minute, I tried to ignore him but his unfaltering and fixed gaze made that an impossible task.

I could not help but look back at him. He gave a wide happy smile and said, "Chai, chai, chai".

I stared back, not comprehending immediately.

"Chai, Chai, Chai" he said again, with excitement and urgency.

I looked past him and saw the snack stall behind him and nodded in realisation. His face lit up and he nodded vigorously and exclaimed, "Chai, Chai, Chai"

From that day on, it became a daily ritual for me. He used to wait for me at the same spot each day and after my little recovery period, I would buy him a cup of sugary tea and a 'pav', the famous Bombay bun. No words were ever exchanged other than his little chant of 'chai, chai, chai'.

In return, I was rewarded with a happy smile and I would begin my journey to work with a little smile of my own. Many would call a man like him, a 'mad man'. I named him the 'Happiest Man on Platform 7'.

I rarely saw him in the evenings as my arrival time to the station was erratic, and the happy man had no way of knowing when I would be there. It just made me feel good that he would probably be at some other place on platform 7 infecting hundreds with his smile. I could imagine so many of those gratified hundreds, responding to his chant and buying him his tea and something to eat. That seemed to be the extent of his desires and wants. It was obvious that his home was the platform and he spent all day moving around its length lost otherwise inside the confines of his mind only to remember his worldly needs when passing a tea stall. There he confronted people like me with the one word that conveyed it all and the one word that he seemed to always say: 'Chai'; Tea. I never heard him utter anything else and that chant was never uttered in a beggarly tone. There was neither plaintiveness nor a request in it. It was just confidently and happily stated, repetitively to us 'so called' sane humans, much like how one would patiently repeat words to a baby, in the hope that she will glean the meaning out of its repetition.

In a sense I envied him. All of us were so preoccupied with our quest to fulfill our needs in life. We go about our daily travails through crowds and bumpy rides to get to our place of work, struggling away through half our day in the hope of a salary cheque at the end of the month.

Yet when it is handed out, we hope that someday that cheque will be larger than the last. With the passing days of our lives we make it a virtue to stay unsatisfied and look forward to the next goal. We are forever lost in this pursuit of this elusive happiness, as opposed to him, who seemed so satisfied with his lot. He yearned for no future, no possessions. His plane of simplistic contentment was higher than any bird even. Birds forage each day, just like him, in their singular quest to fill their bellies. But they too, are bogged down by their needs of finding a mate, raising their brood or guarding their territories. Our happy man was free from every one of these desires. A warm cup of tea and something to eat is all that he asked for in a sanguinary way, and that fulfilled his wants.

One evening, after a particularly bad day at work, and on a particularly hot and crowded day at the station, I was downing a bottle of chilled coloured water from the stall, when I heard him. He was sifting through the crowd and vainly chanting out to the people he singled out, "Chai, chai, chai". I waited for him to get close.

Next to me was a man wolfing down some food and some tea. He was in an avid one-way conversation with the stall owner. Dressed in white from top to bottom, he sported an untucked white shirt and spotlessly white trousers, which ran down to a white pair of shoes. The only colour on him was a smart dash of deep orange that adorned his forehead.

" Today is fasting day," he was saying between mouthfuls. "Every Thursday is fasting day."

" I eat nothing but fruit and drink milk right from morning to evening. None of that, so called, fasting food either. "

" In the evening I first take a glimpse of Hanuman at the temple, offer my prayers and only then do I go home and eat some of that tapioca that my wife prepares in pure ghee."

" Even she is pious. My entire family actually! No one starts the day without a prayer and no one partakes a morsel, before feeding a handful of grass to the cow."

The stall owner nodded away condescendingly, hardly listening, while settling money with the unending number of customers who kept thrusting notes at him of various denominations.

"Chai, chai, chai!" Came the familiar sound suddenly, right behind my shoulder.

Lost in listening to the man in white, I jumped a little and turned around. Happy man stood there with his familiar happy smile. I smiled back and was about to turn around to buy his tea and bread, when right next to me the man in white exploded into a flurry of choice expletives.

He pulled me aside with a large white protective arm and screamed at my Happy Man to go away.

"Chai, chai, chai", the poor Happy Man replied, plaintively and the white man went ballistic.

He screamed at the top of his voice, and despite my futile attempts to rein him in, he rushed at the man, hand raised.

The Happy Man looked furtively from me to him. He looked confused and bewildered. He pointed to me and then the stall.

"Chai, chai, chai" he said. For the first time I heard his tone sound like a plea. A plea not for tea but to be understood.

The White Man swung out at him, missed and cursed.

"Chai, chai, chai", he tried one last time and then he was gone.
He disappeared into the crowd and no one around even noticed what had happened.

I never saw him again after that.

The one thing I can never forget, though, is that through that entire episode with the raving man in white; through the entire time when the Happy Man tried to explain himself with the one word that he spoke, on the face of the onslaught of abuses and threats that were being heaped on him....the smile never left his face.

Watermelon

There are years when the month of Ramadan falls in the peak of summer. The summers in Bombay can be oppressive in a different sort of way than say, the super dry heat of Delhi. The Arabian Sea, along with its breeze gets in bucket loads of humidity that our bodies convert into copious amounts of sweat, drenching one as much as any shower, would. The situation is particularly pathetic at stations where a mass of humanity emanates heat. Here the sea breeze does not get to caress their moist bodies to dissipate the heat into the atmosphere. The air is thick and stagnant under the metal sheeted roofs converting the place into a veritable stinking sauna.

During these times, I have always been amazed how the people go about their daily travails within the confines of the station. Even more amazing are the people who are observing their ritual fast on these days. They go about their day without a single drop of water to satiate their parched throats until evening falls. Then the ubiquitous loudspeakers in the vicinity of the station announces permission to do so, but that too, after prayer. Lesser souls like me, cannot brave a simple train ride without the promise of salvation of a drink from the water bottle at the end of the journey. I can only but wonder at this resolute strength that their faith accords them.

It was one such sultry and hot evening during the month of Ramadan that I stood at platform number 7 on Kurla station mopping up my face continuously, trying in vain to keep the streams of water that leaked out of every pore of my skin, from running down my face to my back and down to my nether regions (I am not sure if I would care to elaborate further on this). The platform, as was usual, was packed to the brim and all around me there were people like me trying to stay as cool and dry as one could possibly be. In times like these, one can best hope to just have one's own sweat running on oneself and not someone else's. So everyone shuffled around avoiding touching each other as much as possible .

The more unfortunate denizens of the platform were there, just like every other day and one could see on their faces; the resignation to the heat and the humidity. Every once in a while, one of them would try to grab a glass of water from the tray laid out on the counter of the tea stall and the shop owner would shoo them away rudely. After all the water service was for the customers and not the filthy urchins and beggars who would contaminate the hurriedly washed glasses that were laid out. I felt sorry for the poor souls; but then, I could not bring myself to offer my own bottle from my little bag for this very same reasoning. This notion of hygiene was conditioned into my psyche ever since I was a child.

The steady murmur and the buzz in the air suddenly disrupted with the call for prayer from a nearby loudspeaker and the crowd stirred a bit. Here and there, some of the people broke away from the crowd and went off. Some time had passed after the loudspeakers fell silent, I saw two young men with tell-tale skull caps come by and clear up some space amidst the chaos. They deftly set up an upturned packing case as a makeshift table and set onto it, three large watermelons from a gunny bag.

Soon there was a small crowd gathered around these two messiahs. One of them briskly and expertly sliced a watermelon into neat thin slices using a makeshift knife, which was essentially a highly sharpened hacksaw blade. The other handed out these juicy red slices with a sprinkling of salt and pepper to eager customers who happily exchanged a five rupee note for each.

I was tempted to buy one too, but on considering the dubious hygiene of unwashed cut fruit on a railway platform (best avoided unless one has the iron immunity!), resisted the urge. Thus resigned to sipping my little water bottle, I watched in fascination as I mentally played out what my mouth and throat would feel like on munching one of those succulent red slices.

I must say that I was impressed by the appropriateness of their enterprise. Added to this was my admiration of the skill that the man displayed at converting this green ball into thin and equal red crescents. This he did deftly and precisely, converting the melon into fifty equal sizes.

A stranger, next to me nudged me with a sweaty elbow and remarked. "Look at these two hoodlums! Five rupees for a thin slice of watermelon! Just making a quick buck after the 'azaan', preying on the thirst of helpless people in this heat."

I shrugged and nodded slowly and continued to sip on my water. Yes...five rupees for a slice of watermelon was daylight robbery alright. The melon could not have cost more than fifty rupees and the fifty slices was a five hundred percent markup!

"Good profit!" I remarked softly as I made the calculation in my head.

A train came by, but it was too crowded and I decided to let it pass. Just too hot! Rather wait for one with a lesser concentration of hominids. I turned again to the watermelon stall. Business was brisk. The second watermelon was already being sliced and the other man was having a hard time keeping up with the transactions as scores of hands reached out towards him.

A little snotty urchin stood in the group staring intently at the fruit. He just stood there, not any higher than the legs of all the adults around him. His eyes moved from the cut watermelon and followed the journey of each slice that went off from the top of the box and travelled to the happy mouth of a buyer. No one took notice of him; not the people, not the seller. Another one of the hundreds of little shabby children that are added daily to the population, borne by homeless and nameless parents, whom no one notices or remembers.

The train had come and gone and some of the buyers had left behind rinds of hurriedly eaten slices on the platform. The waste bin close by was empty and the litter around the stall grew. Some bits of red still hung onto the whites of these discarded rinds. The boy stood around for a while looking and then picked up one of these rinds and with little white teeth, thirstily started gnawing off the remaining red flesh, lapping up the juices that flowed down his chin with his little red tongue.

He obviously was thirsty and possibly also hungry and I could see that he did not stop at the red but ate till he had shaved off the white too. My heart bled at this sight; but one gets immune to these sights as one grows up in this city. Empathy was all I gave him as I watched the scene being played out in front of my eyes as if hypnotised. Done with one, the little boy went on to another. Trains came and went and some more people left behind more half eaten slices of watermelon. As always, when I look back, I wonder if I could have been a better human

15

being. I could have spared a meagre five rupees and bought him a slice of joy. But then, I didn't. This story would hardly be worth narrating if it had ended in that small act of philanthropy.

The crowd had thinned a bit and as I stood around in my stupor, I noticed the watermelon seller cut out one large slice, much thicker than the ones had been selling. He handed it over to the little boy.

'Go on" he said brusquely " Have fun..eat it!"

His eyes showed no kindness. Rather it almost seemed like he was resenting what he was doing. Handing out ten rupees worth of melon. He did not even look at the boy again. Just went back to giving back change to some customer, who had come by.

The little boy took the bright red slice, looking a bit confused. While hesitantly grabbing it, he dropped it on the platform, picked it up again. Brushing off bits of dirt, he stood for a bit staring at the man with wide eyes, who did not look up. Then with a small little smile plastered on his face, he scuttered off, disappearing into the forest of legs that surrounded him, prize in hand. I noticed that he looked back furtively while he ran, almost as if worried that his gift may be snatched back from him.

A relatively empty train pulled up and I decided to get on. I even managed a seat next to the window! I pulled out my bottle and gulped down the cool water gratefully. I pulled up the window pane to let in the breeze as we started to move.

While the train pulled out of the platform, I happened to look out. As my window passed the end of the concrete plinth, I saw the little boy again.

In the scant evening light I squinted my eyes to get a good at his almost silhouetted form.

He was just sitting there and looking out absentmindedly at the tracks. A little girl in a grimy frock, next to him, was hungrily biting into the watermelon and spitting out the seeds.

The Dinner

This little tale is not of Kurla Station. Kurla station is not
the only station in the great city of Bombay, that plays
out little skits of life; skits of daily cruelty and kindness,
sadness and happiness, love and hate and all
such emotions that define us as humans.

My work entails travel at times, and though the norm
is to get onto an airplane and fly off to some place for a
day or two, there are places where one has to travel
either by car or by train.

It was such a journey that landed me at the Bombay
Central Station one night, back from a trip to Surat for
some work. I had taken members of my team to visit a
factory close to Surat and we had travelled by the
Shatabdi Express, one of the good trains of this country.
Throughout the journey, the attendants brought in a
steady stream of food: snacks, tetra-packed juices and
finally a simple and clean tray of vegetarian dinner.

I have never been a big fan of eating airline or train food,
but the pangs of hunger at dinner time and the knowledge
that it would be midnight by the time I would get home,
made me eat up what was handed out.

The meal was simple: two rotis, neatly rolled up in
aluminium foil, some dal, chickpea curry, curds and
some rice. The rotis were thick and doughy and the rest
of the food was tasteless, but then, it was a wholesome
meal and I munched slowly and sated my hunger. I had
not eaten any of the other munchies that had been given
out and had watched, with distaste, as my fellow
passengers swallowed these in a robot like fashion;
eating as a kind of activity to pass time. Over the years, I

have grown to dislike this useless consumption of food that the body had no use for.

Some fellow travellers refused the meal though, and I guessed that they probably lived close to the station and would be able to get home in time for dinner. Since I wasn't that lucky I decided that eating up here was a better alternative to eating at some seedy restaurant in the environs of the station.

My companions got off at an earlier stop and for the last leg of my journey, I was left to myself with my thoughts for company. I started to wonder what happened to all the packed food that was left untouched. The attendants would eat it, I supposed. But then there seemed to be a lot of food and the handful of attendants could not possibly eat all of that. My chain of thoughts was broken by my arrival at Bombay Central and I quickly got up. It was already nine thirty and I had an hours taxi ride to reach home! That too, if I was lucky enough to find one at this hour.

As I had feared, the taxis, waiting like vultures outside, made ridiculous demands of twice the normal fare and so on. I decided to try the app based service instead of arguing with them. As luck would have it, there were hardly any rides showing on the screen. But I refused to give up. After ten futile attempts I managed to book one that showed a wait time of a good twenty minutes. I called up the driver, who seemed to be a nice fellow, who promised to get in as quickly as he could considering the traffic. Traffic snarls were commonplace even at this hour due to the never ending metro construction and road work that had afflicted Bombay lately.

I withdrew to a small patch of road, and decided to wait. Every now and then another vulture would swoop down to ask me if I needed a ride and I would shoo it away. I moved away some more and settled for a place that was away from the entrance to the station and close to the platforms. I looked around. There was no one there, other than a stray cat, some sleeping taxi drivers and a few seemingly homeless people who were sitting around chatting. It had been quite some time since my last smoke and figured this place to be safely away from any of the authorities, to light up a cigarette. I gratefully pulled in the carcinogenic nectar into my poor lungs.

Soon a thin young man in torn clothes, on crutches, came up and sat himself close by, on the wide steel railing that separated the defunct taxi stand from where I stood. He took off the handkerchief tied on his head and carefully wiped his face. His foot was in a dirty plaster cast and he seemed to be in some degree of pain. The cat walked up to him, meowed and rubbed her side on his other leg. He waved it away and then she moved off to seek pleasure from a taxi driver who was sitting on the same railing and eating his dinner. Both the cat and the lame man looked at the taxi driver while he ate.

The taxi driver ate on, oblivious to the two hungry gazes. His gaunt face laboured as he chewed on every morsel that he put into his mouth. I watched, fascinated at how his body seemed to be absorbing the food as he ate. We could never hope to eat with such relish, such a feel of nourishment! Our meals were so mechanical, and when we ate something good, we could only appreciate what our taste buds conveyed to our brains. Our bodies would

21

never participate; feeling the nourishment reach each and every one of our cells.

After a minute or so, I saw one of the train attendants come by, carrying a carton in his hands. I stubbed out my cigarette hurriedly, as it was illegal to smoke in a public place these days and I did not want to get admonished by an attendant.

The attendant walked up to the lame man, looked around, then handed the carton to the man with crutches.

"Eat" was all he said and went off.

I peeked into the open carton with curiosity. It was neatly packed with several rolls of roti in foil and some containers of curry or daal; the ones that had made up my dinner about an hour back.

"Ah! So this is what happens to the leftover food" I remarked to myself, in satisfaction.

The man on crutches rummaged around the box with interest and I expectantly waited to watch him eat.

"That is a lot of food!" I thought to myself.

The box was full of rolls of roti and going by my own standards of appetite, I mentally estimated that it could easily feed four people, if not more. But then my needs of the stomach are meagre compared to these hungry folks, who could normally eat a lot. So I looked on in anticipation, to see if he could. All the same, the food was a lot!

The man kept looking into the box. He fished out a few of the packages, opening them a bit. He put them back again, then looked up at me and asked,

"Uncle, are you going to be standing here for a while?"

I had lit up another, took a large drag and nodded. Looking at my phone, I could see that the taxi wait time still showed twenty minutes and I figured I was going to be there for a while.

"Why?" I asked him, a bit surprised. "Why do you ask?"

"Can you watch over this food till I come back?" He asked matter-of-factly.

"I will go and fetch the old man to share this food. That way, he too will get his dinner. There is a lot here and he hasn't eaten all day...I know that" he said with conviction.

I nodded again and he stood up, winced a bit in pain and then limped away into the darkness. I stepped over closer, next to the box and then surveyed the surroundings to size up my custodianship.

The first to approach me was the cat. She sniffed and meowed and started circling the box. I shooed her away and stamped my feet. She retreated to a distance, sat down on her haunches and meowed in a complaining tone. I kept a wary eye in her direction and she in turn, kept an attentive gaze at me, waiting for me to slacken my guard so she could pounce on the box and get away with the prize. I did not want that to happen. The man on the crutches had asked me to guard his meal and I was not letting him down.

23

My attention was suddenly broken by a light tap on my shoulder from behind. I looked around. It was an emaciated young man in a Manchester United jersey. The cat made her move. I caught the movement in my peripheral vision and stamped my foot again and then looked back at this new man.

He raised a thin finger, pointed to the food box and looked into my eyes inquiringly.

I shrugged my shoulders and shook my head.

"Someone's food. I am guarding it for him. Will be back soon"

The poor man nodded quietly and sat himself a little distance away on the railing. I really was hoping by then, that no one else would approach me. I was hating myself for having to turn away hungry creatures from free food.

Luckily, the man on crutches came along pretty soon. He had led along an old man with him, who walked haltingly in pace with the other's limping gait and had a hint of a happy smile on his face. By the way his cheeks hollowed out every time he spoke to the man on the crutches, I could make out that he was almost toothless.

They both walked up to the box and sat down. Duty done, I stepped back now but continued to watch. The man on the crutches thanked me with a smile and pointed me out to the old man,

"I asked this uncle to mind the food"

The old man looked at me and nodded happily, in acknowledgement. Then they both started to eat; the young man ate with the vigour that I have always loved to watch and the old man slowly chewed with his gums. I watched in fascination, imagining the taste of the food, the texture and its journey to the eagerly waiting stomachs.

The man on crutches spied the Manchester United man, who had stood up by now and was looking at the food intently. The old man too looked up at him and then reached into the box, got out a bunch of rolls and gestured to him to come and take it. The young man came close, sat down and with trembling hands started to eat.

My taxi arrived. Finally!

I opened the door gratefully, to the air conditioned heaven and while getting in, I heard a faint mew. I settled in and looked back out of the window.

The three men were eating silently and the cat was sitting next to them, eating the morsels that the Manchester United man was tossing out to him.

The Surdling

Sardar translates to Leader in Hindi and that is what
Sikhs are referred to as in India; a throwback from the
time when the Sikhs donned their turbans and beards and
declared themselves as leaders and protectors of people
against oppressors.

Three hundred years later that connotation has faded into
the mists of time and the Sikhs of today are variously
looked upon by the rest of the country as overtly large
and warrior-like specimens of humankind; extremely
strong, robust, not to be messed with, or contrastingly as
a butt of flippant Sardar jokes. When the warrior in them
is not awakened, their general jolly nature makes them
good sports and often the best of these jokes are narrated
by the Sardars themselves.

Thus, in some of the more anglicised educational
campuses around the country, Sardars are lovingly called
Surds and the little ones with their yet to grow or half
grown beards, Surdlings!

This little story is about one such Surdling, whom I
happened to come across, one evening on a train back
home.

It was a very wet day. The rain poured down the eaves of
the tin roof onto the edge of the platform, pushing
everyone back to the middle. It was windy too; adding to
the general misery of everyone as the spray continually
drenched the outer layer of people, desperately trying to
shield themselves with their umbrellas. The line of
colourful shields resembled a greek phalanx and the
general din was very much like, what I imagine, a battle
would sound like.

The lined up mass of people emanated a continuous grumble that tried to outdo the constant drumming of the rain and wail of the wind. This was interspersed with the speakers loudly mumbling out announcements of delayed trains followed by sounds of dismay. Occasionally a train chugged in and a company of soldiers burst through the phalanx formation with war cries and flung themselves on the train as if it were a dragon that needed to be subdued.

I realised the futility of waiting for a train that I would be able to get into without getting totally violated in the process. So I decided to travel in the opposite direction to Guru Tegh Bahadur Nagar, or GTB Nagar; two stations away. This was the ploy I often employed on days such as these. Catch an empty train going the other way from the direction of the migrating herds of home goers and alight at a station that is relatively empty. This practice made it so much easier to board the next train in the right direction and also afforded me ample time to settle comfortably and brace myself for the inevitable onslaught at Kurla where the wild eyed, maddened creatures would burst in through the door.

Soon one of these shamelessly empty trains traipsed in on the other side of the platform. I got into a really empty compartment and headed straight to my favourite spot, in the aisle near the doorways. This was the most practical position when one has to travel a few stations and get off rather than make the back and forth journey from the seat area. That day it was raining, making the spot a bit wet. But then it was a small trade-off and I decided to stand there anyways.

There was a man already there. He was dressed in the tell-tale top-to-bottom white, with a caterpillar moustache and

27

a red mark on his forehead, talking loudly on his mobile phone. I found a spot next to him and sized him up. On his neck, hung a heavy looking gold chain and his fingers were adorned with thunky and ugly gold rings. As I got into position, he looked at me irritably, and after bidding a loud goodbye to whoever he was in avid conversation with, he went up and slid the doors shut. After giving me a disdainful look, he came back to his spot.

On one hand, shutting the door was the most sensible thing to do considering the spray from the rain, but this also made the compartment very stuffy and I dare say, I almost felt like sliding the door open again. But then, over the years, one gets trained to keep out of people's way and for a journey of a couple of stations, I resigned myself to the stuffiness.

Much to the white man's chagrin, the door flew open once again just as the train started to pick up speed. A Surdling clambered on to the foot board and hauled himself inside with ease. The man cursed under his breath and started towards the door again, but stopped himself suddenly.

"Hey boy!", the white man barked at the Surdling. "Shut the door will you!"

The boy had just got in and was wiping his face. He looked up at the man and then, without a word, reached out and obeyed. The white man settled back dusting away errant water droplets from his white shirt, still cursing away under his breath.

As with all Sikhs, the boy was tall and of large frame. Even at his young age, betrayed by the few teenage hairs that were sprouting from his chin, his wet tee shirt revealed substantial musculature. As per the traditions laid down by their Guru, generations back, his head sported a tightly wound mini turban ending in a top bun. He clutched a little bundle of books. Probably returning from some class or college, heading home to GTB Nagar, which is largely populated with people of his community. He parked himself on the opposite side of the aisle and stood there wiping himself.

The door rattled and slid open with the motion of the train. The man reached out to shut it again with a loud bang. It refused to hold. He tried the latch too, but try as he might, he could not put it into the catch. The primitive latch was nothing but a piece of steel and over years of use or misuse, was completely bent out of shape. He cursed loudly and retreated after a couple of futile attempts. The Surdling was watching this intently. He calmly walked over to the door and took hold of the latch. I watched him with cursory interest.

The man looked up from his phone. "You need pliers for that, boy. Let it be. You can't do anything about it", he said dryly.

The boy did not pay any heed. Muscles strained and he bent the two millimetre thick steel into shape with ease. His face hardly showed any effort as he slid the piece of metal into the catch. I looked on in disbelief. The white man's eyes moved from the latch to the boy and back again, but then went back to his phone on which he had started to watch some unsavoury sounding soap opera. The Surdling went back to his spot, opened up one of his books and started to read.

By and by, the train pulled into the next station and there was a loud banging on the door. The boy pulled out the latch and opened the door. A dishevelled looking man stumbled in. His head was nodding and my nostrils caught a strong whiff of cheap alcohol and a lot of it. He nearly fell as the train jerked to life and then tottered to the space next to the boy and leaned back. As the train got on its way, he swayed to the motion of the train, struggling to keep his balance. The Surdling did not seem to mind his neighbour and he looked back into his book.

In all of this, the door was left ajar and the white man came to life again. With a loud curse and a blazing look at the drunk, he shut it once more. I smiled surreptitiously.

The drunk stood around for a while and then staggered towards the door. His faltering fingers struggled with the latch for a while and then managed to open it a wee bit and stuck his face out. I could imagine that the cool, wet breeze must have felt nice and was possibly helping clear up his intoxicated head. As the train jerked over a sleeper, the door slid open completely and he almost fell out. We all gasped in horror, but he managed to balance himself by grabbing the bars there. Having found secure handholds, he leaned, his body completely out of the train. As the rain drenched his face and head with the rivulets running down his dirty face, he broke into a song.

I was relieved when the Surdling, reached out and pulled him in. The drunk did not complain but sat down heavily next to the door on the floorboards. He sat there, still singing. His hand reached out and trailed through the curtain of rain as the train sped on. The water bouncing off his palms along with the spray through the open door, landed on all of us.

The man next to me had been watching all of this.

"Hey" he shouted loudly. "Shut the door!"

The drunk paid no heed and did not even look back. The Surdling helpingly reached out and shut it, but the drunk pulled it open once more. I stepped back a bit, trying to keep dry, but just then the rain subsided and it did not seem too bad an idea to keep the door open. I gratefully settled back, breathing in the moist and cool breeze and the boy too gave up his efforts and went back to his book. The drunk, leaned back and shut his eyes blissfully, mumbling something intelligible in-between some lines of song.

All of this was too much for the white man. He banged a fist on the backrest and cursing loudly, lunged towards the drunk and taking hold of his collar, heaved him up bodily. He then shoved him violently down the aisle. The poor drunk flailed around wildly, trying to hold on to some support. Unable to find any, he fell flat on the floor and lay there for a bit with his assailant cowering over him. Having done his deed, the white man looked around victoriously and went back to shut the door.

From the corner of his eye he saw the Surdling stepping towards the sprawled man, helping him up. The man grumbled, but allowed himself to be hauled up.

"Let him be, boy!", shrieked the white-attired man. "Bloody drunkard. Don't help him Let him help himself!"

The boy ignored him and quietly led the shaky man to the backrest, making him lean onto one of the long handles. The drunk, nodding his head, stood there

31

quietly, with a thoughtful frown on his face and continued to sway with the train for a while. He then started to inch towards the door. The White man had just managed to latch the door after a bit of a struggle and now followed his movements with wide angry eyes.

"Don't dare touch the door!" He shouted. "Don't even come near it or else...", he said threateningly.

The drunk did not seem to notice him, went up to the door and started to fumble at the latch. The man was livid by now. He violently grabbed his hand and pulled it down.

But then he did not stop at that. He pulled him from the door and started to push him around, slapping him, yelling all the while. The poor drunk raised his hands protectively and tried in vain, to wave him away, hands flailing in empty space.

"Bloody drunk!", the white one screamed, " Drinking at this time of the day...and getting on the train! I will throw you on to the tracks!"

He shouted out some rhetoric about such people being the dredges of civilised society and how these scum should be wiped off the face of earth. Once he had beaten him down to the floor once again, he looked around exultantly, as if seeking our approval. None of the few passengers took any notice. Such spats were commonplace in this city and no one wanted to get entwined in some unsavoury incident while going about their lives.

The white man came up next to me and looked at my face, searching to see if I was appreciative of his service to society, declared something to all and then went back to the poor soul on the floor. He shook the drunk by the shoulder and pushed him around with kicks, till he crumpled onto the floor once again, his hands held protectively above his head. I looked away, refusing to watch this pathetic sight and also having no intention of getting involved, just like everyone else.

"Why don't you leave him alone", said someone calmly.

I looked up. It was the Surdling. He had positioned himself in between the drunk and his assailant. He stood there towering over the white man, whose head seemed like a dwarfed sphere against the broad shoulders of the boy.

"Just let him be. He is not doing anything to you", he said in a steadfast and authoritative tone.

"Your door is shut now. You are beating him for no reason."

I looked at the white man. He looked thunder-struck and glared up at the boy. The drunk chuckled and hearing this, the man tried to charge at him from the flanks. But the boy stood his ground, and stopped him with one large hand which dropped in front of him like a boom barrier.

The man was fuming by now and his hot angry breaths could be heard over the chugging of the train. He turned his righteous wrath at the Surdling, now. He spat angrily at the boy and raised a warning finger.

"Hey!", he screamed up to his face.

"Get out of the way. Now!"

33

The boy just looked on placidly as if nothing had happened. He looked down at the threatening finger pointed at him questioningly. I could easily visualize him reaching out and snapping that finger like a dried twig.

The man did not stop though. His fury had taken over common sense. He continued to shriek

"Mind your own business young man. Who do you think you are!" he barked.

Every sentence that he spat out at the boy was punctuated by invectives in various languages

The Surdling ostensibly unfazed, stepped back. Keeping the man at bay with one arm, he helped the drunk up and led him onto a seat.

The White Man went ballistic now. " Hey, hey..." he shouted in a warning tone and moved forward.

The people watched in anticipation, waiting for the boy to make short work of the stupid man. But he did nothing of the sort and just continued to shield the now seated drunk.

Another set of rhetoric emanated from the white man. He waved his mobile phone at the Surdling.

"You think you are a hero, little boy! Want to help a bloody drunkard and feel all great! You think you are strong don't you? You don't know who I am. If I make one call, you will get broken up at your GTB station. Just wait and see."

He then addressed another passenger. "This boy. Born just yesterday, thinks he is a hero. Teaching me what to do!"

Thus he went on and on; his rants, (which and I will refrain from penning down here) getting progressively baser and filthier. We all waited for the boy to silence this creature with a laconic blow.

But the young boy just stared back as the man just kept up his tirade. I saw the man take breaks, walk off to the far corner of the compartment and make a few phone calls in between all of this. I could not discern any of the talk, but could hear the words 'GTB nagar'.. 'Sardar'... 'break his legs'.

Thus the status quo kept up until the train rolled into GTB Nagar station. I alighted onto the platform, grateful to get away from the horrible scene.

I watched as the boy heaved up the resisting drunk and dragged him down to the platform holding onto him until the train had left the station, carrying away the offensive man in white.

As the train pulled away I could see the crazed man leaning out of the doorway, waving his and shouting away.

"Come back here, son of a Sardar. I will show you." He called out, even braver now that he was far away from any possible retaliation.

"Just step out of the station. My men will be waiting" His voice trailed off with the departing train. It was a chilling warning and it filled me with foreboding.

I stood at a distance as I watched the boy dial a number as he made the drunk lie down on one of the benches. There was no sign of a train yet, so I waited and continued to watch.

Soon, two extremely large Sikhs with dark blue turbans and flowing beards showed up. I could see their large kirpans [Sikh ceremonial daggers] dangling by straps to their sides. They came up to the boy and started to speak with him. The boy talked, pointing repeatedly at the drunk, who was fast asleep by now, and towards the empty track where the train had once stood. One of the men patted the boy on his back and then led him away.

My eyes followed them up the stairs that led to the outside until they disappeared from sight and I got ready to get into the train which was coming in.

Anu

I often feel that this city has made me, like most people, insulated to others as I pass them by each day. Hence, every wondrous act that I witness, makes me admire the empathy and civility of those few, who have not yet succumbed to the need to shut themselves out from the next person in this city. These incidents make me feel disappointed in myself. But my quest is to get to the office and earn my wage. The need to save time and money makes me hesitant to invest either.

As one of my ex-colleagues, Freddy Bilimoria, used to say: 'Stay focussed on your goals. A sprinter cannot afford to stop and help a fallen runner. He will lose the race if he does so. His goal is to win.'

So I took these words as wisdom, like so many others in this city and went about my life.

It was this same Freddy, however, who was instrumental in me breaking this resolve during the six months while he was my colleague at work.

During the short time that I knew him I grew addicted to his company. Freddy was a Bohemian; a bachelor without a care in this world. Always full of fun and with stories to tell, he was the type everyone would gravitate towards. At the age of fifty, he sported an athlete's physique and in his free time, solved crosswords and mathematical problems for fun. His attitude towards everyone was non-committal, but not in an unfriendly way. He would thus happily treat you to a meal for company's sake, but would shy away from lending you money, for instance. His attitude towards the other

37

gender was interesting too. Always flirtatious and a hit with women, he would nonetheless politely thwart the few who attempted to get close.

Interestingly, he chose to travel by local train and thus became my companion on the way home. Being a man with not a care in the world or responsibilities, yet with a handsome pay package, he could easily afford a car, but claimed to enjoy the thrill of train travel. But then, this was not the only reason.

I soon discovered the other reason for his attraction. Every day, just after we parted ways at the doorway of Kurla station, he would wait a little, then quickly slip into one of the tiny bars that dotted this area. Freddy was a confirmed alcoholic. Despite his many qualities, this was one of his failings. As time went by, I more often than not, started to accompany him.

Just short of being confirmed as an alcoholic myself, in my defence, I did not join him every day, but every other. The couple of shots of cheap vodka (that is all we could afford then), provided the right amount of anaesthesia to brave the travel back home in one of the dreaded compartments of the train, after a horrid and tiring day at the office. But this did not turn to routine due to two reasons. One, was my wish to maintain a facade of decency in front of my office colleagues, who often accompanied us on the journey to the station. The second, the need to get home on time to my waiting family and a stern wife, who perpetually felt that I completely ignored family time.

That evening was one of those days, when we were in the company of a few junior girls from the office. So even though we had time on hand, slipping into the bar was out of question. We walked past these havens of comfort with a nonchalant air; pretending to be listening to the shrill chatter of the girls.

We had almost reached the gates to the station, when someone tugged at Freddy's sleeve and called out. We turned around to see a smallish man dressed in shabby clothes, smiling widely.

"Freddy?", he asked with a confident note.

Freddy looked at him for a minute with a frown on his face. I looked from one to the other, waiting for some reaction, but at the end, there was none. I deduced that Freddy did not recognise this man. He, on the other hand, after peering into Freddy's face for a bit, nodded vigorously and took hold of his hand. He seemed satisfied enough.

"Don't you recognise me?", he asked, smilingly. "Amit...Amit Pawar ...St Ignatius, school?"

At the mention of the school, Freddy looked at him with renewed interest. I could relate to what he must have been going through at that moment. I remember when I have been accosted likewise by some long lost primary school mate.

Firstly, I am forced to search the archives of my brain to retrieve a picture of a boy from school, connect and evolve him to a full grown man who would be looking at me expectantly, as if waiting for me to jump in joy and hug him. Secondly, school days were about thirty years back! I was always surprised when any such old friend recognised me, in the first place. I used to be clad in baby fat then and my features were rather different.

Sometimes, going through my old photographs, I have a hard time recognizing myself!

I saw the conundrum Freddy was grappling with. He could either confess to this sorry man that he had no idea who he was, or could politely shake his hand, humour him and be pulled into an awkward conversation.

The girls had been standing around us at a short distance. They shuffled their feet in impatience.

"Hey. You carry on.", I said to them.

They gratefully waved goodbye and disappeared into the bowels of the station.

I looked back at the two men. In Freddy's place, I would have promptly cut short the conversation. But not him. His bewilderment gave way to congeniality; even though I was pretty sure he had no idea who the man was.

"Wow! What a surprise!", he cried out with the largest contrived smile.

The man called Amit grabbed his hand, yanked him close and gave him a tight hug, while poor Freddy looked at me with consternation and an embarrassed smile. He pulled away hastily and introduced me to the man. I shook Amit's hand with a smile.

My nose caught a whiff of cheap alcohol and stale cigarette smoke.

"Hmm", I went, not really knowing what to say. "So the two of you were school friends?"

"Ah yes! Best buddies, we were! Weren't we, Freddy?"

Freddy nodded with a smile and started to put together as many polite questions that he could come up with which were appropriate when meeting a long lost school mate.

"So, old friend. What have you been up to! Imagine meeting up like this!" he said.

The man called Amit ignored the question and carried on his thread of conversation with a smile.

"Hey, you haven't changed man! I recognised you immediately by your cheeks!"

I looked at Freddy's cheeks. The taut areas on his face were hardly discernible as cheeks. I watched him move his hands subconsciously to them.

"Mmmm...let's sit somewhere and chat", he said, changing the topic abruptly.

We were being jostled around by the hundreds who had no time to stop and resented any hindrance to their destination. A young woman even cursed us and asked us to get out of the way. We stepped to one side and I looked Amit up from top to bottom. Dressed in jeans that did not seem to have been washed since they had been bought , he wore a loosely buttoned shirt through which his white vest showed. I was a bit unsure if I was keen on spending more time with him.

But then, a sudden realization dawned on me. This man had managed to free us of our disapproving companions and the siren song of the bars grew loud and clear.

41

"How about getting into one of these bars?", I asked hesitantly.

Freddy looked at me approvingly and winked.

Amit's face lit up once again with that smile.

"Man, after my heart!", he said happily.

We quickly slipped into the inviting darkness of one of the quarter bars.

Quarter Bars...cheap bars that did not serve by the peg but by the quarter: 180ml of cheap liquor. Pay first, drink after. No discussions, no negotiations and no credit.

The one we walked into was archetypal. Adjusting one's eyes to the darkness, one would find the small counter with a manager, doling out little bottles onto metal trays, held forth by the waiters, patiently waiting for their load after handing cash to the manager. They would then grab a few sealed plastic bags containing fried tit bits and disappear into the darker corners where thirsty customers lurked.

The aluminium, laminated tables were arranged in a row along a passage that led to a sort of toilet. The door sported a sign in fluorescent letters, 'vomiting charge: twenty rupees'. The toilet itself was tucked under a characteristic metal stair, which in turn, sported an arrow pointing to the heavens, saying 'AC'. The steep steps led to the air conditioned section, where each quarter bottle cost about ten rupees more than the non air conditioned ground floor. One would have to adjust one's eyes further and be wary while climbing and duck at the right time under a steel beam, failing which one could crack one's skull. Once up, one had to crouch and make one's way to the safety of a table under the six to five foot high ceiling.

I pointed to the stairs.

Amit flashed his smile. "Ah..five star section! Sure, why not!, he shrugged.

He then paused for a second and turned to us looking worried.

"You guys have the dough?", he asked unabashedly. "I'm cleaned out man."

"Sure..no problem!", Freddy said readily. He was always willing to open up his pockets and in a place like this, one more addition would hardly burn a hole in them.

We managed to locate an empty table in the smoky haze, right under the '*no smoking*' sign and settled down. The waiter came over and stood next to us in silence. We all agreed on a bottle of Romanov: one of the cheap vodkas made with industrial alcohol that tries to garner a semblance of authenticity with the contrived name of Russian nobility. Freddy held out the ransom money and asked for water and I; my usual soda and lemon. Amit said nothing.

As the waiter clinked shards of shattered ice into our glasses, our long lost friend looked Freddy up and down and asked, "So what do you do man?"

"Work at a real estate firm", we both replied. "And you?"

Amit stared thoughtfully into his glass for a bit and then looked up.

"Hmm...nice nice!" he nodded "Nice...Me? I am taking it easy man! Just taking it easy."

I made a mental note that Amit was jobless.

The waiter had attempted to expertly divide the contents of the bottle between the three of us but failed in his estimate. As a result, I received slightly less than a third of a peg and the other two about one and one fourth. About one eighth of a peg remained. Amit reached out and downed it straight from the bottle.

We clinked glasses after the waiter had generously filled up our glasses with water and soda respectively, and after two long sips, went back to our largely one sided conversation from across the table.

After all these years, much removed from one's childhood years at school, one realises that there is not much one can really talk about. People change as they grow up and common context fades into distant memory. Freddy and Amit were probably, if at all, just two students in a class of fifty.

The context of school days, with its incidents, the teachers and the other kids were ancient history. For all practical purposes, two schoolmates, such as them, were as good as strangers. However, some memories do linger, and the two of them tried their hand at reminiscing.

"Remember Edgar?", Amit asked

"No"

"You don't remember Eggy?" … "House captain...hep guy"

Freddy frowned and seemed to strain his memory cells. At the end of his effort it did not seem like any Edgar was stored in there. But he replied with alacrity while reaching out to the plate of boiled peanuts

"Ah yes Eggy...now I remember!"

"He died man"

"Oh"

"Yes man. He had started that business with Shoaib and then they broke up"

I peered at Freddy. He had a crooked smirk on his face that showed that he had scant idea who this Shoaib was.

"Oh!", he said, with an appropriate brow raise. 'Oh' seemed to have become his favourite syllable.

Amit lit up a cigarette, took a long drag and emptied his glass. The attentive waiter rushed in to shake the last drops from the bottle into his glass, only to find it already empty. He stood aside as Amit stubbed out the half smoked cigarette and excused himself to use the toilet.

"More ice. Put more ice" he turned to tell the waiter and then looked at us, with eyebrows raised. The waiter too looked at us, eyebrows raised.

"Get one more", I conceded and handed the waiter the money.

When he was gone, I turned to Freddy.

"Hey. Do you really recognise this man?" I asked

"Not in the least bit!"

"Well, at least he knows that you were from St. Ignatius School, which would imply that he does know you"

"I guess so", he replied. "But what does it matter! Here we are enjoying our unexpected drink. So lets humour him"

"You be a bit careful. Does he not seem like a seasoned freeloader to you? Don't let this get too far"

"Don't worry", Freddy laughed me off. "I won't give him money if that is what you are worried about. I don't give money to anyone. Why then to this sorry chap?"

Amit returned, and wiping his wet palms on his jeans, settled down. "You are cool, man! Both of you. Nice to have met, man"

Thankfully he had forgotten about Eggy and Shoaib, but he threw another one.

"Met Figgy the other day"

"Oh", said Freddy promptly, but then went on to say " Figgy I remember. Used to play the piano. He was something Figuerado. What was his first name?"

"No idea man!"

"Oh"

And thus, the merry conversation went on.

The clock ticked on and Freddy kept pace with the non stop prattle, with his ready 'Oh's. I had finished two drinks already and so held onto the third. Freddy was already on his fourth. Across the table Amit just emptied the bottles as they came. As time passed, the prattle grew slower and slower. By the time Amit looked at us for the fourth bottle, he had slid down to the level of the table. The school friend talk seemed to have slipped to rock bottom as well.

"You know, I got married?" he asked all of a sudden.
"You?"

"No", said Freddy.

"Hmm. Intelligent! But I am not surprised!", he said with a mysterious smile on his face.

He continued while examining his glass. "Well. Fell in love and all that. She got mighty impressed with my fancy bike and my spending. I had money then. Yes. Lots. My old man was rich! I used to smoke 555 and drink in fancy bars."

He took another large gulp. "And then after several months of going around, she decided to run away with me. Her parents never spoke to her after that. They still dont."

"We got married and after a few years, my father died and soon his bank balance too. There were no parties anymore and I had to sell my fancy bike. The bitch then realised that life was not all peaches and cream. She wanted me to take up a job. But I am no good at that. So here we are, three kids, four mouths to feed and no money"

47

"Sometimes I feel sorry for her. She says I have destroyed her life! What the hell! She works as a hairdresser now. Look at her, she wanted to be a writer at one time!"

After this outburst, he went quiet and then after a long pause, looked up.

"Hey can you lend me a bit of dough?", he asked suddenly, shifting his stare from his glass to Freddy.

'Here goes!', I thought to myself.

Freddy seemed unfazed, "How much?"

I looked at him incredulously.

"Five thousand. Even two will do. I will return it next week"

"Hmm...Lets see. Let's see about it later"

I smiled. Classic diplomatic Freddy!

We pretty much drank in silence after this.

A large part of the fourth bottle went into Amit's glass without any water. The waiter had, by now, stopped pouring for us and was concentrating on a new customer who was arguing about something. Amit mumbled incomprehensibly, put his head on the table for a bit and then closed his eyes. When his eyes did open for a bit, he stared up at us with a weak smirk and then turned lazily to Freddy.

"Anu... She was asking about you"

Freddy sat up at this. His eyes lit up with interest.

"Anu?" asked Freddy, his eyes alight with interest "How do you know her?"

"She is my wife, man. My sweet missus". Amit winked and let out a sharp laugh.

With that, his head sunk back again. His hand poked out from under his head as clawed for the bottle in vain and then he went quiet.

I looked at Freddy. His face showed a hint of agitation. He reached out and shook the crumpled figure across the table.

No response.

We sat there for a while looking at him, waiting for him to come back to life. When after a considerable length of time, nothing happened, I ventured to ask, "Now what?"

It was time for me to go home, before it got too late and my wife got suspicious or furious or, both.

Freddy let out a large sigh and shrugged "Just leave him here, I guess. Let me try waking him up"

"Why?"

He did not reply, but tried shaking him again, but all we could elicit from Amit was a few grunts.

"Well, in a way it is better, like this" I said as we finished up our drinks. "At least you won't have to lend him money"

He nodded thoughtfully. Nevertheless we tried in vain for about fifteen minutes. It was getting late. I had to leave now.

"I really have to go Freddy"

I looked around me in the smoky atmosphere. The waiter seemed to have lost complete interest in us and was busy in avid conversation with the new customer. This man was loudly explaining to him, how the government had sold all the important buildings in India to America. A man at another table was telling his friend about his boss's mistress. No one would pay any attention to us slipping away.

"Okay, let's leave", Freddy said, reading my thoughts. "We have paid up anyways"

While I gathered up my things to leave, I saw Freddy reach into his pocket, pull out a wad of notes and stuff them into Amit's pockets.

I have never known him to be one to give money to anyone and had hardly expected him to give money to this insalubrious man whom he hardly knew. But we needed to go away quietly and I did not say anything.

We emerged out of the dingy bar into the familiar jostle after making our way down the shaky staircase. I looked back fleetingly at the still passed out Amit, as our heads disappeared downstairs after having banged mine against the steel beam.

Once out, I accosted Freddy. "Why did you give him so much money? You can be sure you will never ever get that back. Did you see his state!"

Freddy did not say a word as I continued to admonish him for his misplaced generosity. But he hardly seemed to be paying any attention. His mind seemed to be far away somewhere.

We started to head towards the station gates and just before we parted, he turned back to me, put his hand on my shoulder sadly and said,

"It was not for him, friend. Not for him at all. Goodbye" And he walked away.

That was the last I saw of him. A week later the HR department informed everyone that Freddy Bilimoria had left the office.

The Rickshaw Driver

No story about Kurla station can be complete without the onward adventure on the autorickshaw that one has to embark on after emerging from the station doorways. These three-wheeled wonders buzz around like hungry flies outside the gates of the station. They manoeuvre around the hurrying people, cows, vendors, beggars and other unfortunate vehicles that have managed to get into the mess, and then, pause for a second. The crowd pounces on immediately. The technique here is slightly different from the train one.

The goal is to jump into the foot-long opening on one side of the autorickshaw and grab a seat. Only the very athletic ones can get in from the other side. This side has a horizontal bar which one has to vault over and then slide in simultaneously. Every now and then, an inexperienced person who is not athletic enough and without lightning reflexes, tries to get in from that side and is just left behind. Thus is the way, the back seat gets crammed in with three humans and the rickshaw leaves immediately while a super veteran jumps in next to the driver, parking half his backside on the edge of the driver's seat.

For people like me, who are neither athletic nor have an appetite for early morning gymnastics, there is a fenced in rickshaw stand where some of these insects queue up and stop dutifully for the next passenger to climb in. While this sounds very civilized and worked out, the number of rickshaws who ply as such are very few and it is likely that one may wait for hours before one manages to be blessed by one.

I normally wait here for a while and unless the heavens bestow a fantastic stroke of luck on me a particular day, I end up walking to the bus stand inevitably.

That day was bad (like most days). The train was late and I was running behind schedule for a meeting. While getting off the train, I prayed and hoped that luck would shine on me this day. But as usual, my bad luck held and the rickshaw stand bore the familiar desolate look.

I rushed off towards the bus stand almost immediately and to my utter dismay, there too was a long queue and not a bus in sight.

"Just my luck!" I cursed under my breath.

I looked around frantically to see if there were any other rickshaws standing by the roadside who would take pity and ferry me to my destination. I was obviously hoping for too much. These rickshaws were the 'long distance' ones and would never agree to a trip that was less than a hundred kilometers from here. I decided to try, nevertheless. I was really late.

I kept up with my begging and cajoling for a while, until a rickshaw pulled up next to me and asked me to get in. I stepped in with a mixture of apprehension and sanguinity. Once seated, I cautiously told him where I would like to go and braced myself for the preposterous amount he would demand or for him to simply ask me to get off. But I was pleasantly surprised when he did not utter a word, turned down the meter and just set off. I was amazed and though I did not really get down on my knees and weep, I was pretty grateful to this angel who had come to my aid.

As we wove through the market area at breakneck speed, the man spied someone and waved out frantically. He stopped the rickshaw and looked at me, wild eyed.

"Sorry Sir. I need to speak to this man a bit...can I?"

"Sure," I replied.

The office was just a few minutes away and he had made up for lost time already. In any case, I could hardly have refused the man anything on that day, after the service he had done for me.

"It is an emergency" I heard him shout to the other man, gesticulating frantically. I could not really overhear much more than this or any of what the other man was saying.

He got in quickly after that and immediately started the rickshaw. Before jumping to a start, he leaned out and shouted to the man,

"Go quickly!".

I saw his friend wave a hand and nod reassuringly, as we set off again at full speed, honking away in urgency, nearly knocking down a few vegetable sellers. The crowd parted to let us through, and some jumped out of the way, until a red light made us screech to a halt.

I tapped him on the shoulder and gently said, " Brother, no real hurry. I have some time. You need not drive so fast."
The man rubbed his face in frustration and looked back at me. His eyes were welling up and flushed.

"My son, Sir. Don't know what will happen to my son" he said to me in Marathi. "He fell down from the third floor of our building while playing...don't know what will happen to him...Sir."

His voice trailed off, choking.

His unexpected words made me jerk back in surprise. I fumbled for an appropriate reply for a minute. Garnering my limited knowledge of the language, I managed to sputter out in my faltering Marathi, "How is he now? Have you taken him to a doctor?"

He pointed to the back of his head and tapped it repeatedly. "Here...here...he got hurt here...he has been unconscious since then, at the hospital"

A sudden chill filled me up. I was aghast and shocked.

"So what are you doing here? Why are you not at the hospital?" I asked incredulously; switching to Hindi, which is what I eventually do when the conversation tends to get a bit too complex for my limited Marathi.

"Sir...the doctor is saying that he has something called coma. Have to give him injections to save him. Each injection costs eight hundred rupees Sir..."

I accepted that explanation at face value. I was still puzzled. From what he said and from what little I understood about accidents, the poor boy seemed to have suffered a severe concussion and it was quite possible that he would not make it. So what was his father doing driving around all over the city when he should be near his boy!

As he drove on like a maniac dodging everything in his way, he kept talking haltingly between sobs. I could barely hear him over the din of the traffic.

I sat quietly listening to him when we reached my office building. He kept rubbing his face and muttering. I could only make out bits and pieces of what he was saying. He mostly kept repeating the same thing "What will happen to my son...god..what will happen to my son!"

I wondered at the heartlessness of life. Here was a man forced to ply his trade while his son lay in a coma, possibly dying.

However, I realised that I was getting late again. So even though he seemed to have turned oblivious to the fact that we had reached our destination, I got off and started to pay him. He did not reply when I asked him how much. So I read the numbers on the meter and paid him. I was about to turn and walk away, when I stopped. I reached out and patted his shoulder.

"Don't worry brother. He will get better. Have faith." I said, in an attempt to comfort the disconsolate man.

The poor man started to wail at this little show of compassion.

"Look at me Sir...I am not even with my little one...since morning I have been driving around trying to make as much as I can for him. What will happen to my son..Sir!"

I patted him again and turned away. Something made me turn back again as the rickshaw sputtered back to life and started to speed away.

"Wait! Wait!" I shouted out and ran behind me waving my hands. Thankfully he heard me and stopped. I went up to him and handed him the two five hundred rupee notes that I had in my pocket.

The man shook his head disbelievingly but then took the money and reached out to touch my feet. I shook my head, stepped back in embarrassment and quickly turned away.

During lunch break at the office, my colleague smiled mockingly and remarked on hearing my tale, "He probably made a quick buck from you."

"Maybe" I replied dryly

Afterall, in some ways I would really be happier if that was indeed the case!

Three Friends Plus One

On some lucky days one actually manages to get a seat in
the train and this usually happens on Saturdays. On this
day half of the offices in Bombay stay shut, my office
being part of the other half which sincerely believes that
working six days a week increases work output.

On these days, one can settle down and overhear multiple
conversations and zero down and concentrate
on whichever one finds interesting. Helps pass the time.
To say the truth, other than a few, where one cannot get
the context, most of these can be extremely interesting.
The conversations range from personal stories to political
discussion to weather predictions to religion, society and
what not.

Most of these are amazingly imaginative. If one does not
waste one's energy trying to deconstruct these tales and
enjoy them at face value, the experience can be
rewarding. They can really help to pass time and take
one's mind away from the torturous stretches of time that
one has to endure to reach one's destination.

It was one such lucky day and I managed to get into my
compartment and parked my grateful bottom onto a
warm space left behind by some satiated soul.

After the ritual shifting around and minor complaints and
apologies that accompany such interventions, I settled
down. Since I did not perceive any interesting talk
around, I brought out my Kindle to continue with the
book that I had been reading forever. Some people stared
at my toy and one young man enquired if I could watch
movies on it. After my denial he nodded his head sadly

went back to his phone on which he was intently watching some Bollywood movie.

The seats across me got empty as three men got up as the train moved into the waiting station. Normally this was one of those stations where hardly anyone got on and on Saturdays it bore a desolate look. Yet on that day, four men did get on and they headed straight for the seats.

Our side of the seats were filled up and I stood up to let one of them sit as they all seemed to be pretty old. One of them just held me down with a surprisingly firm grip and good naturedly winked at me with a sly smile on his face.

"Not that old son," he said. "These other three. Well they are old and they need to sit"

"Shut up!"cried one of the others and broke into a fit of coughing

"Oh yes! Go on shout. Die of coughing. Just relax and seat yourself," the standing old man laughed and said.

The train jerked to life again and the three settled in, while the one standing, reached up and held on to the luggage shelf above him.

"What's the fun if you don't stand in a local train!" he declared.

He looked down at me with a smile when he noticed that I was studying them with a degree of curiosity.

"Four friends. Thats D'Souza, he cant speak without coughing. Thats Patel; he's rich. Really rich!" He said, placing his hand on their shoulders as he introduced them.

"And your truly is Shinde. I am twenty five and this is Bengali, he has been ninety years old for the last ninety years"

At this all three broke into guffaws which ended up with poor D'Souza, coughing his head off and the one called Bengali, patting him on the back with a quivering hand.

Introductions done, they settled in and started to chat amongst themselves. Every now and then they would laugh aloud, but generally they just excitedly talked. I tried my best to concentrate on my book but old habits die hard and here I had found an intriguing set of people and I could not but help eavesdropping on their conversation.

They all looked well over seventy five or so, excepting for Mr Shinde who looked fit as a fiddle as he hung over from the luggage rack, the popping veins of his arms displaying a decent musculature that must have been formidable when he was young. With closely cropped hair and a french beard that seemed to sit perfectly on his broad chin, he seemed to talk the most and with the most energy. From my reckoning, he looked a lot like an ex army man.

Two of them looked much older, namely Bengali and D'Souza, out of which the latter looked feeble and rundown. His clothes and countenance betrayed lack of success with life and he hardly spoke much due to his cough. His receding forehead, and thin wispy hair never seemed to be in place and looked like they had been cropped at home by a pair of cloth scissors. He had a dirty muffler wrapped around his neck and wore clothes

that hung loosely on his emaciated body, patched up
pants held up by a belt that had missed a few loops. I
noticed that his fly was undone too and when Shinde
pointed this out the group again burst into laughter as
D'Souza apologetically struggled to zip up.

Patel emanated richness in his looks. His shiny baldness
looked manicured and had four long side hairs neatly
combed over to the other side. Meaty looking chap with a
large paunch that spilled over his belt where his belly
button peaked out between the buttons, whenever he
laughed heartily. His fingers sported a large diamond
ring that glinted in the dimness of the compartment.
From their general conversation it was evident that they
were meeting after many years and most of their talk
centered around reminiscing over their adventures on the
local train. They excitedly pointed at every station that
passed and there was always a story to tell at each.

They seemed to have been travelling buddies in their
youth, at the start of their careers in this city which
inevitably starts with local train travel. Some of their talk
also seemed to indicate that they were probably in
college together, but I can't be too sure.

One of their tales centered around Bengali who seemed
to have had a crush on some woman and would help her
out each day and would always insist on the group
travelling next to the ladies compartment, from which he
could quickly get off and on after helping her with her
little bag, which hardly required carrying.

Shinde burst out laughing, "I can never forget your face
when her husband turned up one day and she refused to
even look at you!"

"And what a husband! Six foot three, in a navy uniform!"
"We had to literally haul you up from the platform while you were standing there gaping like one of those fish that you guys eat."

Another roar of laughter and a bout of coughing. And so this went on till they either ran out of anecdotes and memories or the old men simply got tired of laughing and coughing. They then settled down to telling of the turns their lives had taken since their local train days. From what I could make out, that would be perhaps twenty five or thirty years back when these were strapping young men.

Shinde apparently had gone off somewhere in Africa as an engineer on some road work through forests and after coming back had bought a small farm close to Nashik, where he grew Chikoos [Sapodilla] and flowers which earned him a decent income and kept him busy and healthy. His three daughters were all married and settled in different cities of the USA and every year he would spend four months with one of the daughters.

Patel seemed to have done extremely well after he chucked his job as an accountant. He thanked the trains for this.

All nodded in agreement when he stated this. After all he was the one who used to hate the daily travel and the jostling with people. He had bought a small shop in Thane, from which he had started to sell bottles of home made pickles which his newly acquired wife made. Her hard work and skill along with his acumen paid off and soon he had started a large cooperative in one of the nearby villages and his business grew from bound to bound. His son then took over when he was old enough and expanded this to many other foods; a large part of which consisted of packaged pickles and minor food stuff that was supplied to the Indian Railways catering service. That was steady business and nowadays Patel and his wife spent most of their time at his hometown in Gujarat, where he was building a temple.

"Ah! So you finally made money from these trains!" remarked Shinde with a laugh

"And you Bengali?"

Bengali, whose name apparently was Dwaypayan Mukhopadhay (little wonder: they just simply called him Bengali), had stuck to his government job and had retired with a pension. His wife had passed early. So he now lived with his son's family, and enjoyed seeing his granddaughter grow into a young graduate at the Indian Institute of Technology (IIT), Kharagpur. Everyone, including me, nodded in appreciation and approval to this. After all, the IITs were the premier institutes of the country and it was no mean feat to be accepted into one.

D'Souza got up. "I need to get some fresh air," he wheezed out. "The Vashi Creek Bridge will be here soon"

"That's a great idea" said Shinde, " But wait a bit, there is still some time before it comes up. We will all go"

D'Souza hesitated a bit and then shook his head. "Let me go first. There is no one at the door and I will be able to get a comfortable spot. You come later"

Shinde shrugged his shoulders "you sure you won't fall on the way there?"

D'Souza waved him off impatiently and started off while the three went back to their talk. The new topic was about some beautiful girl called Zara, whom they all used to admire and who was a part of their group. The three of them had been madly in love with her and had each tried to woo her in vain. She had just laughed off their advances. And then after she made a move at D' Souza and he thwarted her, she just stopped talking to them. She then went off to Germany apparently married to a German

I looked back at D'Souza who had haltingly made his way to the door of the compartment, which was surprisingly empty and had leaned his back against the backrest. He faced the breeze and looked on with squinted eyes. The twilight heightened the hollows of his cheeks and his gaunt face. His unkempt whiskers blown in disarray, made him seem even more dishevelled than before. Yet his eyes seemed to be defiant and distant as if he was looking into some horizon. His lips seemed to be moving, like he was muttering a prayer. It was hard to imagine what he would have been like when he was younger, when a pretty girl would have chosen to propose to him, singling him out from the foursome. But as of now he looked no more than a tramp.

I turned back from this sorry sight, to the trio, as I overheard 'D'Souza' mentioned while they spoke in low tones. I strained my ears to hear, but could not catch much of what was being said, except that D'Souza apparently now lived in some insalubrious locality. He had even borrowed money from Patel once.

"You remember. He always had money then when we were broke" Bengali said, nodding his head sadly.

"And the women would swoon when he flashed that smile of his" Patel said with a smile.

"Yes. And remember his guitar and that lovely voice of his!" Bengali remarked "He would just hold the show at every party of ours"

The trio was lost in their chat and I in my eavesdropping, when the chugging of the wheels underneath took on a different tone. Cool salty breeze swept into the compartment. The train was already on the bridge by now.

"Hey! We are already halfway across the creek" said Shinde crouching down to the window.

"D'Souza!"

"You did not tell us?" Shinde shouted out to the door. There was no answer.

" D'Souza!". Shinde was screaming now and bounded towards the door as the other two looked on, aghast.

I looked back too.

The space where D'souza had stood was empty.

Across the Jali

The local trains have separate areas for men and women.
These are generally, separate cars altogether, except for
two special ones. In these two, the car is divided into two
compartments, separated by a 'Jali', which is a strong
wire mesh partition painted green in the first class and
yellow in the second.

The first class Jali car of the 8:35 am train that I used to
take each day to Kurla station, happened to be
conveniently located for me to get onto from my
platform. For a few months, until they shuffled the cars, I
had made it my routine to get into this one.

One of the features of local train travel, for the daily
traveller, was that most of the passengers were regulars
and each day one got to see, pretty much, the same
people. Every person would get into the same train, into
the same compartment each day. Most people had their
favourite position, to occupy, too. I had mine too and that
was right next to the Jali that separated us men from the
women. Normally my position in any compartment used
to be, in the aisle right next to the door, where one got to
park one's back and bottom firmly and could keep cool
with the breeze that came in through the open door.
However, during the monsoons, this position turned into
one of the worst spots as one would get plummeted with
rain and get wet.

It happened to be the rainy season during the period that I
started using the Jali car, which proved coincidentally
advantageous. I would head straight to the Jali and park
myself against the same. This offered the desired support
and was still not too far inside so as to make it untenable
to find my way back to the doors at my destination. I

would be lying if I did not also admit that it also offered me a view to the ladies compartment which was occupied by quite a few pretty girls and I looked forward to seeing them each day.

As with all compartments and cars, there were regulars; both on the men's side and the women's. Friendships and even mini clubs formed as always. The friendships gave a more human touch to the travel and kept the sufferers occupied in general chatting during the journeys. People would greet each other, say their goodbyes and reserve places for their friends and alliances. The long journey ones would form breakfast clubs, prayer clubs. The more enterprising ones, who occupied seats would even form card clubs and play various little games on makeshift card tables made of a member's briefcase laid out on the lap.

I have seen these for many years now but always restricted to within the compartment; the men with their own alliances and the women theirs, never crossing over the border wall of the Jali. Even if acquaintances happened to meet across the Jali, the interaction would be restricted to a simple 'Hello' or a wave of hand. Only once, did I see an infiltration of this line of control, and this did not end in the best of ways.

One day when I had climbed in, I found a young man occupying my customary space. This was not unexpected and because I have never really shown much interest in forming any alliances, there was none to reserve the spot for me. I just decided to stand on the spot next to him.

The young man seemed to be in his early thirties, smartly dressed, yet in an unassuming sort of way. The trains were full of such young men and I did not perceive anything in particular about him except for the fact that he was reading a book. These days, a person reading a book on a train to pass time is fairly uncommon. Most people are preoccupied with their phones, watching movies, playing games, chatting, listening to music or simply checking messages and mails. This man did neither. The fairly large paperback was open in his palm while the fingers of his other hand were inserted into the openings of the Jali. Out of habit, a result of my interest in reading, and out of simple curiosity, I peeked in. He was on page number 132 and in the few lines that I could manage to read, the name 'Hari Seldon' featured and sure enough, as I discovered in the days that followed, the book turned out to be first in the 'Foundation Trilogy' by Asimov.

I was duly impressed. A young man who reads on the train, or for that matter reads anywhere at all, is a rarity nowadays and one reading classic science fiction is from an almost extinct species!

From that day on, I saw him each day and every day he stood on my erstwhile spot, reading his book. I did not mind. It was nice to have a person next to me who did not feel the compulsion to strike up a conversation.

It was only after a few days, when I was particularly bored and happened to look again into his book that I realised that something out of the ordinary was going on. The young man was once again on page 132! I looked after another twenty minutes or so and he had not turned the page still. I was surprised and started to study his face with renewed curiosity. That's when I noticed that while his face was transfixed on to the book, his eyes were not. They were directed across and beyond the Jali

.I followed his gaze and my eyes rested on a girl across seated at the window, with a book of her own resting on her lap.

"Interesting", I smiled to myself.

I started to study the girl now. She was particularly pretty in a very Indian sort of way. She was dressed in a smart yellow salwar kameez with a dupatta tied around her neck as is the norm while travelling in trains, where a loose cloth is likely to get snatched away. Long tresses lay flowing neatly from one side of her shoulder down to her lap. Some strands from her forehead kept fluttering out in the breeze which she tidied with her slender fingers, tucking them over her ears. Her large eyes never really looked at the book. Her face was turned towards the passing scenery but every now and then, the eyes looked towards the young man in a quick glance. If they did meet, they drooped down shyly, before moving back to the outside.

My eyes, in turn, now moved back and forth between the two. I noticed that the young man's face flushed every time she looked this way, the colour receding when her lovely eyes turned away. His eyes: they were steadfast and he hardly ever blinked; almost as if were afraid that the microsecond while his eyes shut, he may miss a glance from her. I noticed that the girl gave a hint of a smile every now and then and at this my young neighbour wiped his forehead with a handkerchief vigorously.

I was greatly amused by this cute interaction and this little play kept me entertained that day and the days that followed. Over the days, the interaction grew and soon the furtive glances and hints were replaced by wide smiles and play of eyebrows. A few days later, the girl shifted from her distant spot by the window to a seat closer to the Jali, yet facing it. Asimov and the poor author of the book she purported to read, were relegated to being mere platforms for this sweet affair which I followed closely each day.

As days passed by, and Diwali approached, the train started to get emptier and I found a seat each day from then on and gratefully sat through my journey. Despite my curiosity and interest in the little romance, my need to comfortably sit was greater. I still watched them from where I sat, but never got closer.

The girl had started to stand next to the Jali now and they had started to talk even. I used to watch them regularly separated by the Jali, happily chattering away lost in each other. Asimov had completely disappeared from the equation by now, tucked away in his bag or maybe in some corner of his home. The young man clutched at the mesh with his fingers as always and sometimes she would too. I dare say, I thought I even saw him touch her finger tip.

I particularly noticed her hands, as she held them up. Her long sinuous fingers ended in gaily painted nails, glimpses of which I could catch between the gaps in the Jali. But one detail that surprised me was that she wore the tell tale pair of red bangles and the white one, made out of a conch shell. A detail that told me that she was either from Bengal or Orissa and also revealed that this girl was married. I was a bit taken aback by this discovery, as the young man hardly seemed familiar to her, going by their interactions. He obviously was not her husband.

I was intrigued. One tends to think that liaisons such as these happen in the wealthy classes of society and the poorest. The wealthy ones on account of their wealth and position, are perceived to be freed of the shackles of societal norms and the poor ones; well, they are excused on account of their poverty where every little adventure in life was all that they could afford as entertainment. The girl did not seem to be from either of these classes. Her clothing seemed to be from a relatively expensive store and she seemed to be well groomed; a luxury that the poor could not afford to spend time on. She, obviously, was not rich either; local trains are not used by rich people and continue to be the realm of the middle class and the poor. The middle class of India, as with middle classes all over the world, the petite bourgeoisie, are the ones who are most caught up with society and its norms. A little extra marital affair was not normally what a girl from the middle classes would venture upon. I was quite taken in by the fact that this girl, in all likelihood a wife in an arranged marriage, was emancipated enough in her outlook to dare this affair.

Considering the chauvinistic society here, a man is excused from all transgressions and a man in his youth is expected to be on the prowl looking for adventures, wherever he sees a chance. Having said that, our Asimov bearing young man seemed to have an air of sincerity about him. On the occasional day, when the girl was not there, he would bring out his book but then he hardly turned a page and spent his time staring listlessly across the Jali. Soon, I could surmise , they had shared phone numbers and on days of her absence, Asimov went back into his bag and out came his phone. The pings of messages being sent and received rang continuously.

Then one day she just stopped coming.

By this time, the trains had got crowded again and I was reinstated to my spot beside the young man. He stood there for the next few days thumbing the screen of his phone furiously. I could not help but peek in. Message after message got transmitted but no reply came forth. The messages that had started with a simple 'where are you?' got soon replaced by ones that were more plaintive. Anger replaced entreatment but still not a single reply. The restlessness in the young man grew as he stood there each day fervently looking across the Jali, eyes hoping for her to appear out of nowhere, interspersed with urgent messaging from his phone.

Days passed into weeks and soon he seemed to get resigned to this and after a few perfunctory messages, he would just stop and stare for the rest of the journey. I felt sorry for the young man, but did not dare offer any comfort. I tried, in vain, once to engage him in a conversation about his book. But while he was polite, he did not seem to want to participate in my attempt to keep his mind off the emptiness that was in his heart and across the Jali.

The day right after my futile attempt at his succour, we stood on our spots. A young woman, about the same age as the missing girl, came up to the Jali next to us. The young man was busy on his phone, typing away. As the woman approached, he noticed her and looked up fervently. I could see the hope in his eyes, but then after a quick disappointed stare, had gone back to his phone.

The young woman tapped on the Jali.

"Are you Shyam?", she asked across the Jali. She had a slightly irritated look on her face as if she was in the middle of a very unsavoury situation that she had been compelled into.

The young man looked up again, frowning and nodded, "Yes", he said carefully, his eyes confused.

The train then passed over the Vashi bridge and the noise of the wheels on these suspended tracks drowned all voices and I could not hear what she said then.

But then she did not seem to say much and just handed over a small envelope to the young man and walked away, disappearing back into the mass of women.

Something fell out of the envelope as he opened it up with fervent hands. I pushed aside the many legs in the way and stooped down to pick it up. It was a lock of hair neatly tied in a thin ribbon. I deposited it into his waiting hand, which automatically closed around it. He did not look at me. His eyes travelled from that lock to a little note, that he had taken out of the envelope.

I was curious but , try as I might, I could not discern what was written, but it did not seem like a long letter. Just a note. Maybe about ten lines written neatly on a white paper. The last word, written in larger letters with a flourish said 'Yours Madhumita'

The young man gaped for a bit then looked across the Jali. Standing on his toes, he tried to scan the crowd across. I guessed, he was looking for the messenger and probably wanting to know more. I have no idea what the note said but I could imagine scenarios and by its short length, was sure that it did not contain elucidation to the circumstances of Madhumita's disappearance. Shyam, obviously wanted to know more. I too, craned my neck and surveyed the women across the Jali, but could not locate her either. She had melted into the mass of women in the compartment.

He leapt out of the train at the next station and as the train left the platform. I managed to follow him to the door and looked outside. I could see him running from window to window peering in and standing up on his toes. The train started and he kept up his efforts, jumping up and down, trying to look into the ladies compartment as it flew by. Soon the speed picked up and he was left behind. As the train fled the platform, I could see his lonesome form growing smaller until he vanished into perspective.

That forlorn picture was the last I remember of the young man. I never saw him again and moved back to my favourite spot at the Jali. To this day I wonder about the contents of that letter; did her family discover her secret liaison and she had to call it all off, did she decide that the affair was not appropriate or did she simply realise the futility of it all.

I shall never know but then if I did, would this be a tale worth recounting?

This is First Class

Travel by first class in the Mumbai local trains has its advantages. One gets to rub shoulders with a set of slightly better dressed people and one may be able to argue and fight in English at times. Stuffed between the bodies of fellow passengers in all cardinal directions , one can feel the comfort of getting bathed in the sweat of people of a higher social standing and drawing in the aroma of cheap body spray from the eight armpits that surround ones face, as opposed to pure and concentrated body odour, in the other compartments.

On a lucky day, one might be able to emerge into the compartment more lucidly and on a very lucky day, get a seat even. The seats, too, accord the comfort of hard cushioning and the luxury of having to share the three seaters with two other people instead of getting squished with three as is the norm in a second class compartment. One is also spared the company of beggars, minstrels and vendors and trades people carrying their bags of sharp tools or baskets.

All in all, for the disproportionately higher fare compared to second class travel, the journey is not very different. Most days the compartment is as crowded as the second class one. But, by the right of having paid a higher fare, the travellers feel elevated in status and attitude. Arguments break out more frequently between educated travellers who each have a righteous opinion to human behaviour and etiquette in overcrowded conditions. One can be chastised for getting helplessly pushed onto someone from the back.

At stations when one would think that not even one more body could possibly get into the stuffed compartment, ten to twenty more people just push into the door and just like shaking a can of grains to fit in more, the mass of humanity nudges up and gets volumetrically adjusted.

A wave of admonishing starts off from near the door, travelling inwards into the bowels of the compartment, like a car pile up, as each person steps on the next one's foot or falls onto someone in the process of adjustment. This is followed by grumbles, gasps, groans and arguments. These noises subside in-between stations as the combined mass of people travel on and then as the next station approaches, they start again in the reverse direction as some poor soul tries to reach the door from the seats. Not one person gives way (I dare say, is simply unable to) and if this desperate soul tearing through the crowd is not adept at this, and does not reach the proximity of the door on time, he is swept right back in by a new tidal wave that flows in through the door. People settle in, ignoring the disappointed wails of the desperate failure and grumble as he makes a renewed effort to exit at the next station.

The first class travellers zealously guard this microcosm of theirs. The general order of things is maintained with strict discipline and ethics. Unwelcome additions to the usual crowd are strictly forbidden and illegal aliens are spotted and dealt with, with severity.

Every now and then, some enterprising young boy gets into the compartment with a girl. Now this throws the order of things into complete disarray! Girls are meant to be in the Ladies compartment and their intrusion into the General compartment, though not technically disallowed, is looked at with great distaste. The naive girl, in the throes of youthful love, decides to brave the vice like conditions of the compartment and the possibility of

77

being groped, rather than be separated from her amour for the journey.

As is obvious, this simply adds one extra factor into the balanced equation of the compartment. But then, this is not as simple as that: A girl in the compartment does not take up just one space. General decency or the fear of getting labelled as a gropper forces the men to keep a slight distance and this uses up another half a space and that is criminal in conditions like these and the first class travellers do not let this go unpunished. Grumbles start off all around the couple and some venture further and complain, wondering loudly why a girl would come in there or what has the world come to nowadays. On occasions the one and half space does not help and a poor someone gets squeezed onto the girl and then starts the fight between the girl, the poor someone or the boy and the poor someone. This grows into a huge disturbance all around, which eventually ends in the eviction of the intrusive pair from the compartment, sometimes at their destination and sometimes, well before.

My sympathies, on these occasions lie with the crowd though. As a fellow sufferer, I can empathize with this unwelcome addition and I am sure that anyone would agree, except that this is typical only in the First class compartment and is very rare in the much more accomodating Second class. There, people have nothing to guard and assimilate anyone into their bubble of suffering without a thought.

But the story I am about to narrate, is not one of an amorous couple but a married one, a tiny family.....

The train chugged into Mankhurd station after breezing over the Vashi Creek bridge. We, in the First Class compartment do not really give this stop much of a thought. Mankhurd is typically a station where the section of travellers who get into the Second class compartment wait in anticipation to attack the train. Our compartment is normally spared an assault here and other than an odd passenger or two no one even glances at this door.

As always a platoon of travellers threw themselves at the doors of the second class compartments that day. The crowd was exceptionally heavy that day and craning my neck from our door I could see the mayhem unfolding as the urgency of getting on, grew as the precious seconds passed before the train would jerk to life again. And so it did and as it started off lazily before picking up pace, I stepped aside to allow a young man and a woman with two children as they hurriedly got into our door.

The train picked up pace as we all made space, grudgingly, to accommodate the little family. The young woman had a baby tucked into her arms, its face covered with the end of her saree which she struggled to keep on herself, in the crowd. The young man held onto a girl, not more than three years old, her hair tied into two pigtails with bright red ribbons tied to the ends. I moved my hips to allow a sliver of space next to my legs, so that the little one could get in and not get crushed in the jam.

Once settled in, the man looked around and I could see the bewilderment on his face as he stared from one unfriendly face to another glaring at him. The woman looked equally uncomfortable as she stole nervous glances from her large lowered eyes. From their countenance and their clothes, it was pretty evident that they were not from the city and they obviously had no idea that they had landed themselves into a First Class compartment, unknowingly.

The man was dressed in an untucked white shirt over a set of modest looking trousers. His face was gaunt, sporting the archetypal Indian moustache and his forehead sported a tika [the red dot of powder that all self respecting Maharashtrian men adorn their foreheads with at the start of the day]. The woman was, probably, not more than twenty five, pretty; with large eyes lined with kohl and her long hair tied to a tight bun that had let out some errant strands that had come loose in the melee. She wore an inexpensive looking mangal sutra, the string of black beads that any self respecting Maharashtrian woman wears as a mark to show that she is married. Adorning these beads are one or two little cups of gold. The woman's beads had these cups but then these were possibly some cheap metal plated with gold. Her arms were bedecked with several green glass bangles.

To an unseasoned first time user of local trains, with a second class ticket in hand, it was not uncommon to get drawn to the relative emptiness of the First Class compartment after perceiving the battle charge to the second class doors. Many a poor soul would simply just wonder why no one would get into those empty compartments and just walk in, feeling elated, only to realise the animosity that awaited them inside and for a few unlucky ones, the dreaded ticket checker.

On an office day, no ticket checker in his right mind would normally dare to step into any of the trains, so I figured that they would be spared the large fine, but it was a matter of time before the esteemed First Class passengers would start their attack. And soon enough, it did start.

The grumbles grew louder, and one middle aged man looked at the man and told him matter of factly:

"This is the First Class!"

The poor man just nodded, with gathered eyebrows. I doubt that he even understood what the indignant man was trying to tell him.

Before the conversation could get underway, the train moved into the next station, where about twenty people tried to jump in and the budding engagement got broken up. Amongst the ten that succeeded in their mission, was a middle aged balding man. He slammed into my side and stepped on my foot and settled to my side. Then after a furious struggle to his pocket, which injured me in all sorts of places , pulled out his mobile phone and peered into it. After thumbing around for a bit, he found what he was looking for, selected it and settled down with a satisfied look on his face.

The loud sounds of hymns began to emanate and pervaded all around and the balding man started to move his head to the melodies, eyes closed in devotion. I have always wondered why it was so difficult to buy a pair of cheap earphones and spare everyone, but then listening to hymns in one's privacy does not advertise one's piety. Objecting to this was unthinkable as it was likely to invite reprimand from not only him but from some overzealous persons around, so I quietly resigned myself to relegate this to the background in my mind and instead checked on the little girl, squeezed up next to me. She had fallen asleep by now, held up by the packed legs around her.

Baldy suddenly opened his eyes and spied the young family.

Out came the canned line: "This is First Class."

The young man nodded with wide eyes, seemingly acknowledging this fact of life, being put forth to him.

At this, Baldy started to get hot and he raised his voice over the hymns and asked rudely, "Show me your ticket!"

The young man did not say anything but gathered up his brows and just stared. His wife started to say something, but her voice was drowned as Baldy started to yell to everyone around.

"These Second Class fellows! They happily get into our compartment!"
"Just look at this chap. Not only him; he has got his woman too and his children!"
"We have no place to stand even! And these people do this!"

All around more indignant voices started to sound. Agreement from a few. Sneers from some. A laugh from somewhere.

A disembodied voice from somewhere jeered, "Push them off the train!"

Baldy seemed to take this suggestion quite seriously and yelled at the couple, "Will throw you out if you say anything! Look at the nerve of you!"

The poor man cowered and tried to say something but was just not given a chance. The girl next to me had woken up by now and was staring up wide eyed, alarmed. The baby in the woman's arm started to cry, too.

In all of this pandemonium she tried to calm it down and tried to shout out something at Baldy, but Baldy would not hear any of it and, for that matter, her voice was completely drowned

I put my hand on Baldy's shoulder and asked him to calm down, "Let the next station come, they will get off", I said. "How does it matter?"

Baldy nearly bit my hand and directed his anger at me now.

"Bullshit! Why don't you go to the second class also? What do you mean 'calm down'. Are we not entitled to a little comfort in the mornings!" he shouted angrily against the background score from his phone.

"Why don't all of you jump off !" Someone jeered from the crowd. There was laughter all around.

Baldy went completely ballistic now and broke off to a string of invectives, directed at no one in particular. He invoked everyone's mother, father, sister and any relation he could come up with.

In all of this mayhem, little did we realise that the next station had come up. As the train pulled out of this particularly sleepy little station, to my surprise, a ticket checker got in.

I really wondered at the particular bad luck that the young couple was cursed with, that day. I also wondered what urged the ticket checker to get into the crowded

compartment instead of lying in wait on the platform. From that comfortable vantage he could have lucidly pounced on a few of the suspects.
He made a beeline for the couple without any ado.

"Tickets please!"

He did not even look up as he reached into his pocket and started to write out the receipts summarily, without wasting any time.

Baldy had stopped shouting now. He looked on at the proceedings with anticipation. Eagerly waiting for the inevitable outcome and hence vindicating his ardent labors so far. The compartment, too, quietened down.

The ticket checker looked around with a crooked smile on his face and looking over his reading glasses announced proudly to all

"Wondering why I came in at this hour! I have a nose. Can smell!"

"Shut up" I heard an angry feminine screech break the quietness.

The young woman now came to life again.

She handed her child into her husband's arms and shouted as she made her way to the ticket checker. Her voice was choking and I could see hot tears of anger that rolled down from her blazing eyes onto her cheeks. Her sari had slipped off from her shoulder and she reached into her blouse.

"You want to see tickets, why don't you see them?" She shouted as she thrust a crumpled ticket into his hands.

"Here ...here are the tickets!" she shouted angrily, glaring with her large eyes at all around.

"And all of you keep quiet. Shut up!" She looked around the compartment. "Just shut up!"

The compartment fell completely silent. The only sound one could hear was the chugging of the train.

I looked back at the ticket checker and Baldy peering into the tickets that the woman had handed over and I could see Baldy's face and head grow a distinct hue of red.

The ticket checker coughed uncomfortably. He fumbled with his pen and ticked on the ticket and handed it back to the woman.

I looked around for Baldy. He had melted into the crowd.

The Walking Stick

The door to my bedroom is one of those convenient open closets: in addition to being the place to hang my daily clothes on the cheap clothes hooks that I have fixed at the back, on the floor in the nook near the hinges stands a small collection of brooms and mops, upended as my wife likes to keep them.

Behind this little convenient quiver of household weapons, are some treasures and keepsakes that lie forgotten except on some rare occasions of cleaning sprees that my wife forces me to undertake continually and which I reluctantly resign myself to after months of nagging.

During these times I re discover things and as I reach out at the back, I inevitably pick up this beautiful walking stick. I tend to think, during these occasions, that I look for it and is probably the first thing I pick up. This obviously expensive and classy item stands out not only in its beauty and impeccable craftsmanship, but also in its incongruity to my otherwise humble possessions.

Yesterday was cleaning day and I found this little treasure of mine once again. Brushing off the dust summarily, I picked up a polishing cloth and pensively ran this up and down its rich dark shaft of heavy wood, which ended in a black metal ferrule, equally solid in feel and appearance. The handle; a beautifully worked silver knob, cast into the likeness of a predatory bird head, held to the shaft with a monogrammed golden collar.

The monogramme read W M O D.

Of all the unlikely places, this priceless treasure came into my possession quite by chance, on the humble platform of Kurla station. No. I did not find it and nor did I steal. It was given to me.

It was one of the usual evenings at the platform and I stood at my usual place near the tea stall. I recall it to be winter because I remember it being quite pleasant and people were not crowding under the few fans and were spread out. In this city winter translates to 'not hot' and this is the season that every visitor from anywhere in the world can bear to visit the city. The few tourists this city receives, come during this time. The corporate travellers schedule their visits during this time as well. For us denizens it means that the train compartments are not musky with odours and the shirt which one wore after the morning bath still smells fresh by the time one reaches office.

Anyways, I was waiting for my regular train. I had reached a bit early and out of habit did not feel like taking an earlier one. The pleasant weather did not make it an unbearable wait and I decided to buy a hot cup of sweet tea from the stall and was slowly sipping it, surveying my surroundings through the steam that rose from my cup. The usual set of beggars, vendors and the motley group of commuters stood around. Over the ambient chatter, one could hear the calls of vendors, muffled announcements and the continual blare of train whistles. Trains came and went and the crowd got thinner and thicker. One of the earlier trains streamed into my platform from the southern end and as it left my gaze as I followed it to the north.

My eye fixed on a very unlikely sight then. The platform offers the strangest of sights when one really looks, but most of these sights are somehow not unexpected. One almost finds it natural to see one legged people, beggars of all shapes, appearances and sizes, fighters with bloodied noses, dogs, cows, harrowed office goers, stylish women in short skirts and militant ones with stern faces, etcetera. But one never expects to see nobility on a wheelchair being led into this place by a stylishly dressed young man.

The sheer inconsistency of the appearance of the pair in the surroundings of platform seven of Kurla station, fired my intrigue and interest. The man on the wheelchair looked to be in his late sixties, by my reckoning. At one time he must have been quite a decent looking chap and I dare say he did not look too bad at this time either, with most of his features framed by a generous and manicured white beard that flowed wispily, almost to his waist. A few sparse white curls escaped out of the french artist's beret that he wore on his head. (It was only later did I notice that his hair was largely tied back into a very thin white pony tail that dangled from the back of the beret).

The man, in his prime, must have been a pretty strongly built person because even though age had wasted his body down, he did not seem frail or feeble in any way. I wondered if he really needed a wheelchair or was it his ostentatious societal lethargy which mandated that he be taken around by someone, in public places such as this.

The old man was also dressed very well! He sported a smart pair of obviously expensive trousers, on which he had put on a tailored khaki jacket on a spotless white shirt. The fading twilight glinted now and then on his highly polished black shoes as his chair navigated towards where I stood. Carelessly laid across the handles of the chair was the beautiful walking stick, his fingers drumming on the knob as he looked around.

The young man wheeling him about, was in obvious discomfort. He did not seem like a servant or a valet, but rather a son or a nephew. For some reason, I decided that he was a nephew; a young nephew who had probably attended a public school or some of the pretentious schools of Bombay. His attire spoke of boutiques, subtle and expensive, styled by some of those atrocious designers that one gets to see on TV. He seemed to be more interested in dodging the hoipolloi and treading with care on the platform floor, rather than in the piloting of his old uncle. He looked furtively around at his surroundings and jumped a little, every time a train sailed into the platform. It was amusing to watch him. The poor youth seemed like he firmly believed that he was being given a guided tour of hell. Every now and then he would glare down at his uncle's head and angrily curse to himself.

The alien pair slowly came very close to where I stood and then the old man signalled his nephew to stop. He looked around and his eyes met mine while he studied my surroundings carefully. His tiny bright eyes, peering out under the long white hairs of his wrinkled brow sent out an invisible request and I found myself moving over to make him space. He said something to his nephew and he in turn got his uncle right next to me.

The old man started to inspect the place again. He looked up at the announcement board, at the ancient fan, the tea stall, the bench, the platform number; nodding at each, almost as if he were ticking off a mental checklist. After this careful inspection, he gave a satisfied nod and an excited smile played on his face. He looked at me and smiled. I smiled back. He looked away and nodded again to himself.

In contrast to his nephew, I was struck by the fact that the old man seemed to be completely at home with his surroundings. His eyes did not show any distaste or surprise with anything he saw. Rather they betrayed an almost happy look of recognition, when every now and then they would fix on some portion or element on the platform and I would spy a hint of a smile on his largely hidden lips.

He suddenly picked up this walking stick and prodded his harrowed nephew.
" Arjun. Arjun!"

The nephew frowned down at his uncle indignantly and pleadingly.

" You can go. Ask Sushil to drop you to the nearest Uber point and ask him to get the car back to where we left him."

The nephew looked at him in horror. " Why have you come here? I swear ya...what a place!"

The uncle grimaced in exasperation at this, but said nothing and then smiled sardonically.

" And now you want me to leave you here! What if someone robs you or something!" The poor dear bleated out in his classic south Bombay accents.

" And you want to be there to save me! Haha", grunted the old man, turning to look at me with amused wide eyes.

" See this young man here?", he said, pointing at me, much to my surprise, "He will save me"
The old man nodded again, reached into his pocket and brought out a leather covered hip flask, opened the cap and stopped short of putting it to his lips.

"Run along now. Go. You will die of something here. Go carefully and don't forget to tell Sushil to keep the car ready...and tell Sheetal that I will be home late...not that she will notice anyways." He waved impatiently with his walking stick.

The nephew gave me a helpless look. I nodded as reassuringly as I could. But he did not look too convinced. But his uncle did not look like a man to be disobeyed and I am sure, at the back of his mind, he was happy to leave behind his mad old relative in this crowded hell; get away as far away from here as possible and think of this as a real bad dream.

The old man took his swig from the flask as he watched his nephew leave and giggled at his nephew's scream when the platform dog came up and sniffed at him curiously. Then he looked up at me and winked. I smiled back again. I was beginning to like this man. His regality and confidence was magnetic. Coupled with that was his strange level of comfort with the platform environment.

My train came by and I was readying myself for my leap, when I felt a prod on my butt. I looked back. The old man was holding up the walking stick and looking at me.

"Young man...my protector...can you help me get out of this stupid wheelchair," he half commanded.

I hesitated a bit. My train was there. But then I decided to just help the old man. I was, after all, very curious to see where this was headed.

He stood up with almost no help from me. It was, like I said before, a compulsion of his societal standing and age that made a bit of help a stylish hobby that he could afford to ask around.

As he stood up he leaned a bit on his walking stick, "Thank you young man!" He exclaimed with the confidence and exuberance of a person, one sees in people of a certain degree of standing in life, in society.

He looked around again and spied the feeble beggar who was stationed in his usual spot, restricted from moving around much because of one missing leg.

"That bloke could do with a wheelchair. What say, young man?" he looked at me. I nodded slowly. I must confess I did not think very highly of that particular statement. It is so easy for a rich man to say things like this carelessly; almost in a callous manner.

I gathered up my courage and started to stammer something to this man but stopped. I realised that he seemed to have suddenly grown oblivious to everything and he seemed to be peering above his half moon glasses into the crowd that was descending from the northern foot-bridge.

The bridge was not teeming with people as usual, but there was a fair number of people making their way down the steps. Polished to a gleam by a million footfalls each day over years, one has to be habituated at negotiating those and an inexperienced person coming down these, immediately stands out.

93

I looked too, at the bridge and could immediately spot the object of the old man's attention: a middle aged lady was gingerly making her way down the steps, carefully going a step at a time and looking up every now and then at the platform. To add to her obvious discomfort, she seemed to be also lugging down a large suitcase, with great difficulty.

She stood out in the crowd, not only due to her awkwardness, but also by her distinct clothes. Even from a distance their styling and choice was obviously different from the crowd that hurried past her.

The old man suddenly looked back at me. "My dear young man," he said, "May I ask you for one last favour?"

I was actually surprised at this change of tone, so unlike his earlier commands, to what seemed, to be an earnest request. I nodded again.

"Thank you so much," he said, shaking his head excitedly. "You see that beautiful girl coming down the bridge? Can you please help her down and get her here!"

Reminiscing now, I smile in amusement. I just started off towards the lady. Neither did I bother to confirm with the old man, if this indeed was the correct 'girl' that he intended me to help and fetch, nor did he, in his visible excitement, reassure himself if I had understood. Something made me sure that I was right and something assured him that I knew who he was talking about.

I made my way through the crowd using my years of navigating experience and soon wormed my way to the lady. I greeted her summarily and offered to help her with her large suitcase down the steps, to which she readily agreed.

Once down, we both stopped to catch our breath. She thanked me and was about to start walking off; so I introduced myself and told her about this gentleman who was waiting for her and who had sent me over to fetch her. She looked a bit surprised and looked at me for a bit, and then excitedly in the direction that I was pointing. She reached into her purse and after rummaging for a while, fished out a pair of stylish round glasses and put them on urgently. I spied that her fingers were trembling a wee bit as she did this.

While she was doing this, I sized her up. She must have been in her late forties. Her long salt and pepper hair fell stylishly around her shoulders, right to her waist and framed an unusually attractive face. She was dressed in a beautifully tailored black dress that stopped just below her knees that gave way to an expensive looking pair of stylish shoes. Draped over her bare arm was a jacket that looked too warm to wear in the so-called winter of this city. She had an air of confidence about her and she stood there peering over the crowd, comfortable and sure of herself even in her attire that was completely incongruous to Kurla station.

"My good man!" she addressed me in heavily accented English. "Where is he?...cannot see him"

"Right there madam." I pointed again towards the old man "right next to the tea stall; there"
She looked again, holding up her glasses with her long fingers, which I could not but not notice and suddenly her face lit up and she almost whispered to herself, "There you are. My god there you are!"

95

After that there was no looking back. She just strode off towards the tea stall, seeming to have completely forgotten about her expensive heavy suitcase that she had left behind with a complete stranger.

I looked at the suitcase. There were airline tags pasted all over. 'Lufthansa' shouted out the tag that was secured around the handle and by the looks of it, the suitcase did not seem to have been even opened after its obvious retrieval from the baggage carousel.

I hurried on behind her and easily caught up with her despite her head-start. Afterall, in spite of her apparent ease with the environment of the platform, she seemed to be a bit out of her depth at making her way through this surge of humanity. She soon fell behind me and that made her journey easier, with me cutting my way through like an advance guard, leading the way.

Within minutes we had reached the old man who seemed to be just staring at her, completely unconscious to anything around. His eyes were transfixed at this lovely woman and there was wonder in his eyes. I tried hard to see if he would smile, or hold out his arms but he did nothing of that sort. Just stood there, eyes blinking rapidly.

His lips opened and closed, mouthing some words that only he could hear. She, on the other hand, was beaming. I can never forget that dazzling smile! It was, I must say, a beautiful smile. But what struck most was the joy that it exhaled.

She reached out at him and wrapped herself around the old man's quivering frame. He, almost immediately, untangled himself in obvious embarrassment and held her at arm's length. She broke into an amused twinkling laugh and shook her head happily. Her dazzling smile never left her face and her eyes never left his, as she brushed off some imaginary dust from his jacket. The old man just stared at her and then shook his head a little, as if waking from a trance.

He looked at me as he gathered up his wits and reached out for the suitcase from my hand.

"Thank you, young man!" he said. His commanding tone back. "I will take it from here"

I mumbled a "You are welcome" and obeyed.

The woman turned to me and with her beautiful smile and said kindly, "Thank you so very much Sir. It was so kind of you to help me"

I nodded. I am sure I blushed even. I distinctly remember a slight temperature filling up my face and started to back away.

The old man turned to me and handed me his walking stick. When I looked at him in incomprehension, he grunted carelessly, "Won't be needing that no more, young man!"

And with that they started to slowly walk back towards the bridge.

"What about the wheelchair?" I called out to him.
"That poor bloke without the leg....give it to him, young man" he called back to me without even turning back. I looked down at that beautiful walking stick, much as I look at it now, and then looked back to their backs disappearing into the crowd slowly.

Yes, I forgot to mention: he did say something to her as he held her off and she vigorously nodded in happy conviction.

He said something like: "You came! You actually came…"

Unfortunately I did not catch her name.

But I do remember that there was a musical tone to it, when he said it out.

The Boy

Every morning the train that I take crosses the Vashi
Creek, running precariously over the single track bridge.
I look forward to this breezy journey over the waters.
While the passengers right inside get a mere whiff of the
salty wind, those next to the doors can just shut their eyes
and stop breathing; the rushing air filling up their lungs
automatically. If one opens one's eyes, one is greeted
by the rushing of the rippling water, several feet
underneath. The compartment falls silent as every poor
soul drinks in this elixir, before the train chugs into the
mainland and the arms of the waiting hordes.

Sadly, many a times this lovely respite can be marred by
a particularly callous act by some of the passengers.

As the train gets onto the bridge, one often encounters
some person flinging a single-use plastic bag containing
flowers and left over food : offerings to the Gods. Often
these also contain disposable plates and glasses. This is
the new age version of an ancient custom.

It is sacrilegious to throw away leftovers from a 'puja'
performed into the dustbin where the sanctified and
hallowed items would mix with garbage and waste. The
proper way to dispose of these, is to fling them into a
river or the sea. Since this city has no more than a
glorified drain termed a river, the sea is the proud
recipient of these offerings, charged with conveying
them to propriety by its tides.

In older days, one would make a trip to the sea side and
pick a deep spot to throw these. But in these days of
corporate jobs and attendance machines monitored by
Human Resource Departments, such free time is a rare

luxury. A convenient ride on a train across the deep creek presents an obvious opportunity each day of a person's life. The day following any festival or holy day, sees scores of hands reaching out into the wind and letting loose the contents of their bags. More often than not, bag and all. These offerings fly happily along the length of the train before gravity carries them into the waiting arms of the sea.

On such occasions, one has to be careful not to lean out of the door or risk the possibility of being hit in the face by a speeding flower or worse still, stale foodstuff or even the odd coconut.

I always imagine the fish feasting on these goodies as they rain down from the heavens. I am not sure if fish eat flowers, but well, I guess they break down soon enough and feed some creature or the other or simply fertilize the seabed and the shore where a lot of these wash up, eventually. Such has been the custom for hundreds of years and as opposed to earlier days, when only the fish near the shores would get lucky, nowadays deep sea fish too get their blessed share. The sea and its life have grown used to these food packets.

But sadly, not the plastic bags. These multi-coloured flotsam can be seen bobbing on the surface and gathered along the shores, making the creek look like a garbage dump.

It was a day after one of the many dozen holy days of the year. I found myself at my usual spot with my backside planted firmly on the backrest next to the door, facing the wind. It was a lovely day. I could already feel the cool saline breeze caress my clothes as the train got into Vashi station. Once it took on the load from this stop, we would emerge into openness before getting onto the bridge.

My immediate neighbour was a stereotypical office-goer, with his backpack hung on his chest. I noticed this with a feeling of distaste. An unsaid decorum while travelling by a local train is to either stow away the bag on the overhead rack or to place it next to one's legs on one's feet. This allows the people packed around one to stand comfortably. However, nowadays, many people smugly hung these on their chests, making them resemble kangaroos, causing discomfort to all. This practice obviously offered them constant surveillance of their bag and also ensured a one- bag distance from the next person.

The train started to move and a thin young boy jumped in and found himself a spot on the opposite backrest. He made himself comfortable and placed his small colourful haversack next to his feet. He plugged in his headphones, placed them on his ears and his eyes got transfixed on his phone, thumbs furiously typing away. His head bobbed with the swing of the train and to the music in his ears, that could be faintly heard even over the loud ambient sound of the train, the crowd and the singing wind.

I entertained myself inspecting this young man while he stood oblivious to the rest of the world, and noticed that his neighbours kept casting occasional distasteful glances at him. Lost in his little world of friends and networking sites and probably headed for one of the many colleges in the city, he seemed to care less for these stares.

He looked distinctly non-conformist. His dreadlocks fell well below his shoulders and the wind blew a few errant locks in all directions. His face was barely visible, but

101

one could still catch the occasional glint from the sunlight bouncing off the tiny studs in his earlobes in between the locks. The rhythmic movement of his chin which was lined with a youthful bunch of hair, betrayed chewing gum.

His tee shirt proclaimed: 'DON'T WORRY, IT'S ORGANIC', written with a bold flourish over the outline of a cannabis leaf. He wore torn jeans that revealed patches of hairy skin. Every now and then, his hands would travel to one of these and he would carelessly scratch. I noticed that he was wearing cheap rings on all fingers barring his thumbs. Each ring was different; one was a snake, one a leaf, one a simple band with runes and so on. Some fingers even had two bands.

My kangaroo-like neighbour had been staring at him too, for some time now. He moved closer to me than he already was and started to say something to me in undertones. This is another annoying habit of some passengers, who refuse to believe that strangers may not be interested in chatting with them. I certainly found it annoying to be jerked out of my pleasant reverie as he let loose his lips. Thankfully, the noise in the train made it impossible to comprehend what he was saying, but I gathered he was saying something about the boy as his eyes kept moving from my face towards his.

"What?", I asked with a bit of irritation.

He mumbled something again looking quite irked, too. I could not hear a thing and felt very pleased about that.

As luck would have it, the train suddenly stopped, just as it was to get onto the bridge. There was a collective cry of dismay. The boy looked up too. He fumbled into his

102

shirt, fished out a peace pendant hung from his neck and started to chew on it. The chewing gum in his mouth got stuck to it. The boy pulled out the pendant, inspected it, nibbled it clean and put it back into his mouth.

The man next to me realised that he could now be heard and attempted to strike up a conversation once again.

"Look at him!", the good man elbowed me while pointing to the boy and as I shifted uncomfortably.

"Must be eating up his father's money on booze and drugs!", he sneered disapprovingly. "See the way he is dressed. This generation has gone to the dogs."

I shrugged my shoulders and tried to look away, praying for the train to start again. But his fingers grabbed my sleeve and tugged for attention.

Just then the train jerked to life and everyone heaved a sigh of relief and the man's sentence got drowned. I rolled up my eyes and shook my head at him, but the man was persistent. He almost placed his lips on my ears and spoke loudly.

"Look at his hair. Disgraceful, isn't it?"

I looked at him in amusement. The middle aged man was balding and was obviously not too proud of the fact. He had taken great efforts to hide his bald patch by combing over a few long strands of his hair across his scalp. The sea breeze was playing gaily with these strands and they were fluttering away, upright.

"Are you jealous", I could not help but blurt out.

The man gave me a look that nearly incinerated me to ashes. I decided not to pique him further and went back to admiring the sea. He realised that it was futile to engage with me and so started speaking to another man next to him, who seemed more receptive and appeared to concur and empathize with him. They both took to whispering into each other's ears and casting occasional acrimonious looks at the boy. I could overhear bits and pieces of the conversation and it mostly dwelled on decrying the present generation and their complete disregard for our values and ethos.

The boy still took no notice of him or anyone for that matter. Soon he had languidly slid down into a slouch as he continued to chew on his pendant.

I saw the man next to me screw up his face in obvious distaste. Having found an ally, he gathered the courage to speak up.

"Which college do you go to?", he now addressed the boy, raising his voice. "Why don't you stand straight?"

The boy must have heard something over the music, for he looked up from his phone, stared through his round framed glasses. The corner of his mouth twisted to a hint of a smile and he winked at the man. Deed done, he went back to his phone.

This tiny affront to the good man's ego was not taken lightly. He righteously looked around to all around him and started off. Finding me to be the most convenient person to direct his wisdom to, he spoke to me again, much to my consternation.

"No respect for our traditions and culture. Look at him, he is almost standing on his books"

"There was a time our boys prayed to Goddess Saraswati before setting out for the day's study. They prayed to books and behaved. Look at these boys now; no care for anyone, no care for the world, disrespectful of elders. I bet he talks back to his parents, spoils innocent girls, drinks, smokes."

He addressed the boy again loudly, "Going to college, huh! For anything but studies, I'm sure."

The boy looked up with an insolent smile playing on his face and nodded vigorously, and the man grew more livid. The man upped his ante and broke into a string of sentences, which the boy completely ignored. I just looked away in irritation as the righteous man's rambling got relegated to the background noise.

As the sea crept under our feet and a few flowers started to fly by, a man stood up from one of the seats. He left behind his backpack on the seat to mark his reservation of the same. Having confirmed this with fellow passengers as his witnesses, he gingerly staggered past the people towards us. All made way to let him through. His forehead bore the tell-tale tika (the holy mark) and in his arms he matter-of-factly carried a large translucent plastic bag, stuffed with flowers, some disposable glasses and bowls, which showed through. Hidden away, I guessed, were also tit bits of the myriad items and eatables that were the leftovers from a performed puja.

The men next to me and his new found ally obligingly made space for him to come to the door. The man positioned himself and brought forth the plastic bag.

I saw the young boy look up from his phone. This time around, the mocking smile was replaced by a look of interest, intent and purpose. He looked at the man, his eyes transfixed, following his every move. He came to life as the man raised his hand to throw his blessed luggage off the train, into the sea. He rushed to the door and put his hand on the man's shoulder.

"Uncle!", the boy called out, his youthful voice raised over the din of the wind. His pendant fell back to his chest.

The man stopped and looked back at him inquiringly, eyebrows bunched. He stared the boy down, from top to bottom.

"Please don't throw the bag", the boy beseeched him. "Can you not just empty it out."

"Don't throw the plastic bag and the cups, please"

The compartment suddenly hushed up. The people around looked at both in suspense. Eyes moved from one to the other, expecting the man's indignated retort to the impunity of this unsavoury young man, who despite being half the man's age, had still had the audacity to advise him!

My neighbour now exploded.

"Hey hey, young man!" He cried out, placing himself between the two with an acrobatic jump.

"You are speaking to someone who is old enough to be your father. Do you know that? You were born just yesterday. Speak with respect! What do you know or care about our customs!"

"Ignore him Sir. Please go ahead. The train will soon pass the bridge.", his ally said to the man with the plastic bag. "Do what you have to do. This boy would never have said a prayer in his life. What does he know."

"Boy, keep quiet and go back to your phone" my neighbour turned back to the boy

The boy did not even look at him. His gaze at the man with the plastic was unfaltering.

"Uncle please, don't throw the plastic bag."

The man looked at him and then at my neighbour. He hesitated, looking a bit conflicted and confused. Then he broke into a lovely smile and looking at the boy, nodded his head resolutely. He then looked at my excited neighbour, placed a hand on his shoulder and gently pushed him aside. My righteous neighbour had just begun to say something, but he stammered and shut up. This was something beyond his understanding and he seemed to have no idea how to deal with this situation.

I had not noticed that the train had stopped again. This time right in the middle of the bridge.

The man with the plastic bag did not say a word. He reached into the bag and started to empty its contents into the breeze, his lips moving in silent prayer. The flowers flew in all directions like a celebration and my nostrils caught the whiff of incense and camphor. A happy smile lit up the boy's face and he sank back to the backrest.

"Thank you uncle!" the boy said gratefully before going back to his phone.

The man was now carefully emptying out each disposable ware and stuffing them back into the plastic bag.

The train sprung back to life just then and the man turned to go back to his seat. As he passed by the boy, he stopped to pat his head gently, drawing a shy smile from the young lips.

I turned to my chastened neighbour. He had finally been rendered speechless, much to my relief. He stood there with a strange look on his face, looking defeated along with his equally perplexed sympathizer.

As I looked back at the young 'insolent' boy, I found my hands break into a clap which was taken up by the whole compartment. They cheered at the man with the plastic bag and the young boy.

The boy looked up and acknowledged me with a smile.

Looking back, I always liken that smile to one I had seen in college, on a poster of one dreadlocked singer.

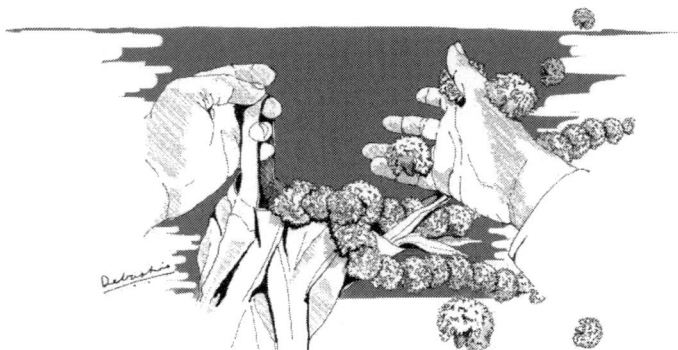

Anjum

It is often said that Mumbai never shuts down. Home to
thousands of businesses and enterprises; these function
tirelessly and relentlessly, through the year. Even during
public holidays, many offices stay open and one sees
office goers hurrying along as usual. Having said that, the
crowd does get sparser as many offices including the
government ones, banks, schools and colleges and the odd
private office observe their holidays religiously. This
makes it a pleasure to travel by the local trains on
these days. More often than not, one can easily travel
seated. They even offer the opportunity for some women
to venture into the men's compartment and travel with
their male colleagues.

It was Janmashthami, the birthday of Lord Krishna. Our
villainous office decided to stay open that year, much to
everyone's dismay and irritation. The entire city of
Mumbai celebrates this occasion by suspending colourful
pots from impossible heights and waiting for the teams of
human pyramids to come along, take up the challenge to
reach these and bring them down. The city is famous for
this ritual tourney. If a team does manage to reach the pot,
they are rewarded with a grand prize. Music blaring from
loudspeakers set up at every road junction adds to the
festive air and brightly dressed people wait in anticipation
to cheer the teams.

In the midst of this gaiety, I set out for office with a feeling
of great disinclination. Robbed of a holiday I knew very
well that it promised to be a futile day at the office since
the other offices we needed to deal with, would be shut. I
cursed the Human Resources Department and our bosses
who took great satisfaction and pleasure to tick off an

additional day of attendance of the year. However, once out of home, the vexation got thrown to the wind and instead I derived pleasure by comforting myself, on the joys of travelling in an empty train.

The day turned out to be as fruitless and pointless as I had imagined. At the strike of the evening bell, the entire office gathered up their belongings and ran out of office, relieved to be done with the day and looking forward to going home with a slim possibility of enjoying what remained of the day. I too, was in a hurry to go home but then Maya asked me to wait for her.

Now when Maya asked me to wait I could hardly refuse. She was attractive, pleasing and really good company. Always with a story to tell and very loquacious, she made me look forward to my journey to the station whenever the chance arose. She was one of those in an office who everyone gave tasks to, because of her efficiency, capability and eagerness to work. Thus, even on a day like this, when no one really did much but just sit around, Maya had something to wrap up.

When we finally managed to get going, I was so pleased to find a line of auto rickshaws waiting for us right outside the office gates. We actually had the luxury of choosing one and I climbed in happily after her. Maya, as always, entertained me throughout the ride. She was recounting an anecdote with alacrity and I listened with rapt attention. However, by the time we alighted at the station gates after a, much too, swift ride through the relatively empty streets, the tale was not finished. I remember feeling a tad disappointed that the auto ride had ended so quickly.

As we walked into the platform, we paused at the spot where the Ladies compartment stops and as always, I bid her goodbye with despondent air.

To my pleasant surprise, she shook her head with a smile and suggested, "Why don't I come with you into the general compartment? Today the trains are completely empty after all"

"Sure. Why not", I replied with a seemingly nonchalant shrug, yet feeling very pleased secretly.

The train came into the platform almost immediately and we both scrambled into the nearest compartment and found ourselves in the one that was divided into two: the ladies and the men's. Surprisingly there were no seats empty but other than a couple of people near the doorway, the compartment was devoid of any other standees. We made our way to the meshed partition and took up our place there.

"Hello!", cried out an oddly mannish voice from the ladies' side. I looked across curiously. Seated in one of the seats across, was a gaudily made up figure who was looking intently towards us with a large lipstick lined smile. I looked closely and realised that she was a Hijra; a term for transgenders here. I rolled my eyes and looked away to avoid further interaction. It was not uncommon for a Hijra to call out to people teasingly. That was a tactic they often used while begging, relying on people's discomfort to extract alms. I have learnt to ignore them over the years

"Hello how are you", Maya answered back with a degree of familiarity.

I turned to her surprised.

111

"Don't engage her Maya", I cautioned her condescendingly, noting her naivety

She gave a twinkling laugh and waved my apprehensions off, "That's Anjum. She is my friend."

The transgender stood up and came over to the meshed partition now and the two of them started to chat. When Maya introduced me to her, she gave me a winning smile and gathered up her palms into a greeting. I mumbled out a hello of sorts, not quite managing to veil my unease.

"So today you are in the men's compartment?"Anjum's large kohl lined eyes widened and they gestured towards me and back with a conspiring look. She danced her neatly plucked eyebrows at Maya with a teasing smile. I turned a distinct shade of purple at that suggestive look.

"Tchaaaaa! Anjum! Nothing like that." replied Maya, brushing her off with a laugh.

"Hmm. Okay. But he is a good one."

Maya shook her head in exasperation and then they both broke into a laugh while I stood there flabbergasted.

"Why don't you come here too? Today you can." suggested Maya. To my relief Anjum shook her head.

"Mens compartment! No. Someone is sure to misbehave. Anyways, I have to get off at the next station. We have a party today at one of my friend's home"

"Lovely. Enjoy yourself! That's why you are dressed so beautifully today. Now I understand"

Maya winked at her,

"Friend?" It was her turn to move her eyes and raise her brow and they both broke into a hearty laugh once again.

They chatted for a while, Maya admiring some of Anjum's jewelry and vice versa, until the next station came up. Anjum bid her many goodbyes and after waving at me perfunctorily, she got off.

I looked at Maya questioningly. She noted my bewilderment and smiled benignly, "Let me tell you about Anjum"

This is the story she told me:

I remember the day I first met Anjum. It was the day we got that rare bonus from the office and when I hopped into the ladies compartment, I had a spring in my step. I was so happy. The compartment was crowded, but not so much of a squeeze like it can be at times. I normally do not stand near the entrance, but that day, I decided to do so and enjoy the breeze. I was feeling blissful and content and started to sing to myself, oblivious to the people around me. As you know, I often do this, to pass time. I picked a particularly favourite song of mine with a catchy beat and was soon lost to the world

"Darling, you sing beautifully" I was broken from my reverie by a masculine sounding voice; a surprising thing to hear in the ladies compartment.

I looked to find Anjum smiling at me. She was dressed in a colourful saree and was heavily made up, with deep coloured lipstick on her lips and her eyes lined, much like how you saw her today, except that she wore flowers in her hair that day in place of that colourful headband that she had worn today. I distinctly remember the jasmine

113

flowers in her hair, because their sweet smell reached my nostrils.

I had got a bit startled and stopped singing. My instincts made me alert and wary. She cocked her head at this with a crooked smile and said, "Darling. Don't stop. I was really listening to you"

I was surprised. I always sympathize with transgenders who are subject to ridicule, harassment and cruelty in our country. But I have never really liked the way they are wont to force their way into your private space, say crass things and make lewd gestures, until you succumbed and paid them something to just be rid of them.

Anjum did nothing of that sort. She stood looking into my face amicably for a while, eyes twinkling. When I did not go back to singing, she started to sing herself. She sang the same song that I had been humming and I noted that she sang it really well. I nodded in appreciation and she smiled and walked off, still singing. She went around the compartment. She stopped briefly near everyone and if one did not give her money, she just moved on to the next. Far from being a nuisance, or clapping for attention, she just carried her song from person to person hoping for some kindness in return. I noticed that most people handed out some.

That day on, I saw her often on my way back home. No one seemed to mind her and some, including me, started to look forward to her sweet singing. Except for a grumpy few who looked askance at the presence of a Hijra in the compartment, everyone grew to accept her as an essential feature in their daily travel home. The nasty ones would shoo her away or even be mean to her and say something rude. I never saw Anjum talk back. She would smile and quietly walk away. Everyone liked that about her.

She grew to be so familiar that soon the regulars, other than giving money, gradually started to become friendly with her. They would offer her food, some would discuss clothes or hair and some would even share their family problems. I too often gave her money. I am not one to hand out alms to beggars normally but I reasoned that she could possibly never get employed anywhere and sadly this was her only livelihood. Yes, one thing I remember; I once offered her chocolate. She loved that and told me that she had almost forgotten what it tasted like from the time she was little and with her parents.

But what we shared the most were songs. After she had done her round of the compartment, she would come to me last and then we would sing something together, standing near the doorway. Her singing had one interesting aspect to it; she could sing in both male and female voices pretty well and I used to enjoy doing duets with her. We sang together almost on every journey until she got off at some station. No one seemed to mind, except for the inhibited ones who would frown upon us. We used to ignore them and Anjum would at times blow a kiss towards them and cause them to get flustered and look away.

One evening while we were standing next to the door singing we noticed a young girl standing very close to the door. She would not have been more than twenty five and was dressed in fashionable but decidedly affordable clothes. Her proud possession seemed to be a very new looking phone on which she was incessantly chattering away with some friends. She carried a large handbag which rocked from her forearm, swinging out of the door even.

It all happened in seconds. She stumbled and let out a scream. I rushed towards her and managed to stop her from falling out. Holding onto her we both collapsed to the safety of the floor. Through the corner of my eye I caught a glimpse of two men on the tracks as the train sped on. One was wielding a large stick at the end of which hung the handbag which he had managed to snatch from the young girl's hand. I looked her over to see if she was hurt. Getting one's bag snatched from one's hand with a stick while speeding on a train could have caused grievous injury. A lot of people rushed to us and one portly lady knelt next to her to check on her and was relieved to find that she seemed to be unhurt.

The girl was crying loudly but I guessed it was more from shock rather than any physical harm. One kindly lady offered her some water as I tried to soothe her.

"It's just a bag girl. Thank god you did not fall out. You are safe now.", I said. But she was inconsolable. She just kept shaking her head and her anguished crying grew louder.

"I had a thousand rupees in the purse!" she wailed "what will I do now! I have to give that money to my mother....and...and" she trailed off as she suddenly started to grope around her pockets and look around.

I realised that her phone was not there too. She started to cry even louder, "My phone...I just bought it today. I got my salary and decided to buy a new phone. What will I do? My mother will kill me."

I really felt bad for her but was at a complete loss as to how to help her out.

116

Pulling the chain was of little use, as the men would have been long gone. One lady promised to report it to the police at the next station. We all knew that while this was the proper thing to do, it hardly would make any difference. The young girl's money and phone were gone forever.

Everyone felt so helpless. Advice and sympathy poured in from all directions yet those were just words and did little to actually help the poor girl. During all this, I had completely forgotten about Anjum and I suddenly heard her voice, humming some song to herself softly. I was taken aback. The last thing I expected from her was this degree of apathy. She seemed to be lost somewhere, seemingly unconscious to all that was going on. I could not contain my disappointment and consequent resentment at her when she decided to come towards us, smiling benevolently at the girl, who seemed to retreat from her approach.

"Tell that Hijra to leave that poor girl alone." shouted out one of the women from the background. "How dare she have that smile on her face!"

Anjum paused. Her eyes moved to the women and she gave an uncharacteristic glare at them. Then she looked back at us. I got up and stood in her way protectively shielding the girl, with a defiant look on my face.

She gave a short haughty laugh when she saw me do that. I felt her strong hand on my shoulder. Anjum gently pushed me away and sat down next to the girl. The young girl looked up in fear and suspicion at her.

"Anjum!" I cried out. She took no notice.

She patted the girl on her head lovingly. The girl shivered.

Then without a word she reached into her blouse and drew out a bunch of notes. She carefully wrapped it into a neat bundle in her dainty handkerchief and put it into the hands of the girl.

"Thats all I have. Should be about three thousand.", she said.

The girl looked at her disbelievingly and hesitated. But Anjum puckered her lips into a kiss and smiled at her kindly and urged her with a nod and she took the bundle in a robot like fashion. She managed a 'thank you' in a choking voice and her tear stained face broke into a shy smile.

The train had stopped at a station by now. She stood up and stepped off into the platform and while leaving she looked back at us. As her eyes met mine, she gave me the saddest of smiles I have ever seen.

After that day I did not see her for a long time. She completely stopped coming to our compartment. One day while I was waiting for a train at Kurla, I bumped into her. She tried to avoid me, but I ran after her calling out her name and she stopped. I threw myself at her.

"Anjum, I am sorry" is all I could blurt out as I burst into tears. She held me while I cried on her broad shoulders. "Please come back and sing with me....please, please." I kept repeating.

She held up my face by the chin, looked into my eyes and smiled, "I will darling, I will", and the next day she did.

We have been friends ever since.

Maya decided that she had finished her story and she looked at me and smiled. I looked out in the direction of where Anjum had gone and then back at Maya.

"But all that money? She could afford to give all of it? Just like that?" I asked incredulously.

"Well, many days later, I asked her."

"What?"

I asked her, "What about you Anjum? How did you manage after giving away all that money?"

"What about me darling? I am used to not eating for a few days since the day they took me away from my parents." She laughed and said. "Now lets sing."

I stared at Maya and said nothing. We were quiet for sometime until I turned to her and said,

"Someday I would like to hear the two of you sing Maya"

"Why not!" replied Maya.

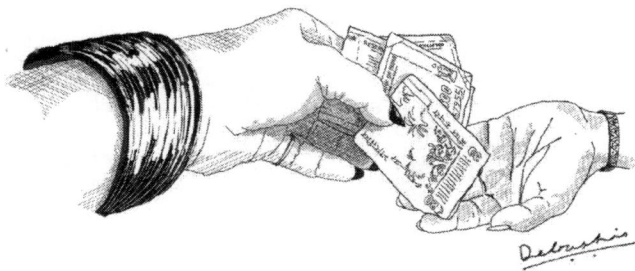

How to Chew Gum

It had been a while since I had stopped my travel by train to work. I had finally saved up enough money to add to the traffic snarls of Mumbai; deciding to elevate my status. I had thus waved out symbolically to Kurla station on my last journey home, and at my home platform, at the train as it left the station.

I was relieved to put behind me those frenetic days, the long waits, asphyxiating squeezes, the drenching rain, the bumpy auto rickshaw rides and having to live out of my backpack. I had got myself a shiny office bag and traded all of those travails, with long traffic jams, expensive fuel and the incessant motorbike dodging. I slowly got addicted to the comfort of my small air-conditioned car and my private time listening to music despite the fact that my travel time now increased by a full hour. My family time was considerably reduced due to the congested roads and also due to the fact that I was unable to get out of office on time as the excuse to catch a particular train back home was no longer valid.

Funnily, I did miss the train travel at times. On Saturdays, when journeys by train tended to be relatively bearable, I would make my erstwhile customary trip to the station by rickshaw and proceed to do my day's travel by train. This became an interesting interlude that I continually enjoyed.

One has to realise that one cannot simply decide to walk into a local train. One has to be prepared. One can draw a parallel to Arnold Schwarzeneger in one of his action movies, where there is an essential scene where he grimly puts on war paint, wears his fatigues, ties a bandana and adorns himself with an array of grenades, serrated bow knives and picks up a ridiculously large gun. Then with a resolute expression, sets out for the impending battle.

On trains too, one has to wear the right clothing; toughly stitched clothes that can resist crumpling and ripping and shoes that wouldn't get dirty when stepped on. The backpack is another must; one with many compartments to safely stow away one's wallet, and the survival kit consisting of a water bottle and packed lunch. Some train warriors would keep their mobile phones in the backpack alos, but I had mastered the skill of keeping mine secure in the front trouser pocket, along with some loose change for paying the shared rickshaw drivers. Thus prepared, much like Mr.Schwarzenegger, one would take a deep breath, tighten one's jaw, put on a resolute look and set forth from home

On a particular Saturday when I had gone to the office by train, my boss announced that I had to urgently make a trip to some godforsaken place. I thanked my stars that I was dressed in train gear that day as the easiest and quickest way there would be to take a train from good old Kurla and get off at a station called Titwala.

This was about sixteen stations away and I calculated that by the time I would reach, it would already be quite late in the day. Despite my attempts to convince the boss to shift the voyage to the next Monday because of this, I soon found myself on the train and braced for what was to come. To add to my woes, in my hurry to get on the train, I booked a second class ticket via my phone.

So there I was in the unfamiliar surroundings of the second class compartment. To my relief I found it to be sparsely populated. This was possibly due to the fact that I was getting on at noon, when the office rush is long over.

I ventured towards the seats and realised, to my dismay, that they were already occupied. I cursed my misfortune and steeled myself to endure the long journey, standing. I was pleasantly surprised when all the three occupants on one row of seats squeezed themselves to one side without a word, when I came close. They managed to disoccupy about three fourths of a seat. One of them gestured at me to sit.

This behaviour is specific to the second class. I remembered one of my friends telling me about this. The first class snobs would zealously guard their right to the seats and never bother to accommodate an extra person on the three seaters. The regular humans in second class suffered no such pretenses. Every three seater was occupied by four people and no one seemed to think much about this.

I squeezed into the little space thanking the other occupants, who just stared incomprehensibly at me, probably wondering why I was thanking them for such an obvious arrangement. I gratefully made myself comfortable, plugged in my earphones, thumbed my phone and after selecting a good track, settled down to survey my surroundings.

The seat across had six occupants. A man, a woman, three young girls and a very small boy who sat right in the middle, half seated between the laps of two girls. They looked like villagers and were obviously a family. I surmised that the family was of a very typical configuration, that was common to their class. The couple and their relatives would have considered the birth of the girls, a misfortune. The husband and wife would have taken a long break at their yearly acts of procreation before gambling over the sex of the next child. And then, after a wait of a few years, and probably tons of prayers, pilgrimages to holy shrines and penances, they would have taken another shot at it. Their prayers had been answered and the husband would have made a quick trip to the closest family planning center and laid to rest any further possibilities of adding another hungry mouth to the dinner pot.

The daughters must have been around twelve to fourteen, in all likelihood, a year apart. The boy, about five. Their mother seemed quite young by regular standards to have such grown up daughters, but this was not surprising. Most girls from poorer and rural sections of the population here, get married off at a very young age and I would not have been surprised if the woman had been married off at the tender age of fifteen even. The law of the land, handed down right from the time of our British colonizers, forbids this. But such laws are mostly ignored amongst the sections, who make up most of our population. As with most laws here, enforcement is rare.

While I was entertaining my brain with such analyses and deductions, I happened to notice that the little boy was staring at me. The way he looked at me, made me feel as though I were an alien from outer space who had landed on his home planet. I winked good naturedly but he did not react. He kept staring without blinking; a feat which most babies and really small children are capable of. I tried smiling. Finding no reaction to that either, I looked away from his steadfast gaze, which made me a bit uncomfortable while I tried, in vain, to concentrate on the music playing in my ears.

Now is that not the most difficult thing to do! When you know someone is looking at you, you cannot just look away for any length of time. You feel a burning sensation on the side of the face that is being looked at and your mind urges you to look back. I gave in to that urge and found his large eyes still fixed onto me.

"What the hell!", I decided. Two can play a game.

I ventured to stare him down too. I peered into his eyes but was hardly a match for him. Soon my eyes started to water with the effort, and I was forced to blink. I renewed my efforts again and again and thus went on our little game, until I threw in the towel. I, obviously, stood no chance. Instead, I started to study the little starer.

He was dressed in a neat little shirt with some sort of patch animal sewed onto his front pocket. He wore cotton half pants and his chubby legs ended in bright red socks. His shiny black shoes were off and I could see them dangling in the hands of one of the sisters. His spiky hair had been oiled down to a gleaming shine and had been combed with a side parting. Another sister held on to his colourful little hat which had a cartoon character printed on it. Both his ears were pierced and sported rings made of an extremely fine wire of precious metal. Possibly gold.

Having inspected the boy and having tired of the staring game, I turned my attention to the girls. In comparison to the neatly dressed little critter, they were dressed pretty plainly. Two wore very cheap looking identical frocks with floral patterns and plastic slippers on their feet. The third, probably the eldest, was dressed in a yellow and green salwar kameez made of shiny cloth. A shocking pink dupatta made of some shear semi transparent synthetic material, hung across her shoulders. For girls of their age, they hardly wore any form of jewelry other than a few odd trinkets made of plated metal and plastic beads.

I noted another archetypical state of affairs here: spend all you can on the prize boy child and ignore the girls.

I realised that I was getting too judgemental here. I turned my mind from such thoughts and reached into my pocket for some chewing gum.

Chewing gum is something that I had formed a habit of only recently after I quit the cigarette. I had realised that the money I saved, not buying my customary packet of cancer each day, was enough to allow me to spend on expensive chewing gum. And so I indulge in this little luxury, to this day. I brought out the packet of Wrigley's 5 after rummaging around for a bit and carefully opened up the packet. Something made me look up at the boy now. At long last, his eyes had stopped looking at me and were curiously surveying the little black packet in my hand.

The shiny beady eyes followed each movement as I opened up the flap and drew out a stick of gum. His brow was faintly bunched now and he looked intently at the stick. He shot a quick glance at me and then looked back at it, frowning. I wondered if he frowned because he was surprised to see a grown up man bring forth chewing gum from his pocket or because he just did not recognise the thin stick for what it was. I smiled triumphantly. I had managed to get rid of that stare at last!

I was about to unwrap the stick and convey it to my waiting mouth, when I felt a little bad. Afterall, here was a child and it was hardly proper for a grown up to chew candy and gum in front of him while he would just watch. I reached out and handed the stick over to him. He retreated immediately into his older sister and shook his head, frowning at me. The sister, who had been lost in her thoughts, looked down to see what was going on. She spied my hand and wrapping her arm around her brother smiled shyly at me. The younger one, next to her, looked at it longingly and hesitantly reached out. A quick admonishing glance from the father made her withdraw immediately.

I attempted to offer the gum to the boy once again. The father was watching. He looked at me and smiled. He said something to the boy, in a dialect that I did not recognise, and nodded his head. The boy took the gum apprehensively and glared back at me. But then that was all that he did!

Gum in hand, he just sat there as if not very sure what he was supposed to do with this alien gift of mine. I smiled and gestured with my eyebrows but his frowning gaze was back and he just stared at me. His little hands were fiddling around with the stick on his lap and he even dropped it once. He tugged at the sister's dress who did not take any notice. The father immediately said something to her, and she obediently retrieved it from the floor and after wiping it on her dress, put it back into her brother's little hands.

I must have waited at least a good five minutes after that. But the boy just sat there. I decided to fish out another piece and began to unwrap it. The boy looked at my hands again and followed them closely and then looked down at his own stick. Slowly he started to fumble and then carefully unwrapped it and tossed the paper to the floor. I dramatically put my gum in my mouth and watched with satisfaction as he watched me do this, and followed suit.

Once the gum was in his mouth, he froze again. His eyes started to move up and his brow bunched up with concentration, but his mouth did not move. I waited again but he was back to just staring at me, and rolling up his eyes once in a while, as if lost in deep thought.

I grew impatient. I started to chew harder making sure that my mouth moved conspicuously. His eyes shot to my lips and I saw his little mouth move cautiously and his face lit up slowly. Soon, the frown was gone and he started to chew with gusto. I settled back, feeling fulfilled in my venture and satisfied that I had got rid of that offending stare.

I decided to reward him. I reached into my bag, fished out a chocolate bar that I always carry for nutritional emergencies, and put it into his hand. He looked curiously down as his fingers closed around it. As before, he did not attempt to open it and just showed it to his sister quickly who nodded and then looked away. The father had dozed off by now and the boy shot a quick glance at him and quietly put the bar away into his pocket.

He did not look at me for the rest of the journey and amusingly, I actually started to miss his gaze! Every now and then I would glance sideways to see if he would eat the chocolate. But he seemed to be busy chatting with his sister.

The family got off at the next station. The sister helped him put on his shoes and taking his hand firmly, led him towards the door. My eyes followed them. While they waited for the train to come to a halt and the father was busy looking out of the door, I saw the little boy tug at his sister's sleeve. He quickly slipped the chocolate bar into her hand. She bent down to ask him something and he pointed towards me. I saw her look at her father nervously and surreptitiously slip the bar into one of her pockets.

Just before she stepped off the board and helped her brother down, both the boy and the sister looked back at me and he gave me a lovely smile. I smiled back and waved.

Such smiles are the ones that I always remember particularly whenever I reminisce about my journeys on the Lifeline of Mumbai. Those are representative of the little joys that people who are still human, glean out in the midst of the most miserable situations.

Incidentally, that happened to be my last journey on the local trains of Mumbai and I am happy that it ended in a smile.

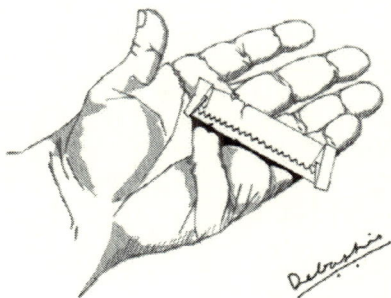

Before you check Google and Wikipedia

Bombay and Mumbai
This city on the Arabian Sea is the capital of the state of Maharashtra and the financial capital of India. Once a sleepy group of seven islands, it was christened Bombay by the Portugese and then gifted as dowry to the British. The colloquial name for this has always been Mumbai and by and by the state fought tooth and nail to officially name it Mumbai.

Kurla Station
One of the first stations in India, set up in 1853, made by the British, who used to call it Coorla. The present environs are perhaps the most congested and messy areas in Mumbai. This has inadvertently become the main station on the Harbour Line and the Central Line that is nearest to Bandra Kurla Complex, the new business hub of the city.

Harbour Line
The main local train lines are the Western Line, the Central Line and the Harbour Line. The newest trains run on the Western. The second hand ones on Central and the third hand ones are passed to the Harbour Line. The Harbour Line was so named as it connects all the stations that serve the eastern coast of Mumbai that has the harbour.

Rag Pickers
India has a wonderful track record of recycling. Everything from newspapers to bottles and any odd thing that is thrown away are collected and recycled. An army of souls are engaged as the collection machinery. These humans, armed with a large sack and improvised poker, set out each day to collect tons of recyclable bits and pieces that are strewn all over the city and deposit their

load at collection centers and earn a paltry sum to feed themselves.

Mad women and men

Mentally ill people amongst the poor sections of the society are a burden to families who can barely feed themselves. They are cast out and except for the ones who find a shelter home, live off and on the streets or find shelter in stations, bus stands, etc.

Chai : Tea

Tea is the national drink of India. Barring a few states in the south, who drink coffee, tea is drunk by the rich and the poor. It is called Cha or Chai. This egalitarian drink is made at homes and is sold in tea stalls. In Mumbai, the roadside Chai is made from powder tea, in a mixture of milk and water and laced with kilos of sugar and a dash of ginger and spice. It is served in tiny glasses and has become one of the quintessential features of city life.

Pav

This unique soft bun has it's name derived from the Portuguese word 'pao', meaning bread. It has been absorbed into Maharashtrian cuisine as an accompaniment to a wide variety of curries and also the covering of the famous Bombay Burger or vada pav.

Fasting

Fasting is a great and old tradition of India and its implication varies between religions and regions. It ranges from not partaking any food or drink during certain days to eating uncooked food only to eating only specifically sanctioned food items to just a change from their regular diet.

Daal and Roti

Daal is a cooked soupy dish made of various lentils. Together with Roti which is a simple Indian flat bread it forms the staple for most of India. Thus in the Indian context 'Bread and Butter' is replaced with 'Daal and Roti'

GTB Nagar

The Koli community were fisher folk and one of the original inhabitants of Mumbai. One area where they were concentrated in was Koliwada [abode of the Kolis]. This place was slowly inhabited by Sikhs who adapted their tandoori knowledge to the local fish giving birth to the famous 'Fish Koliwada'. Soon they outnumbered the local population and the place was re christened Guru Tegh Bahadur Nagar, named after the ninth of the ten Gurus of the Sikhs.

The Nihangs- Sikhs clad in blue

Nihangs belong to a clan [or sect] within Sikhism, who still adhere to many of the warrior customs from the time of the 9th Guru. They are conspicuous in their navy blue turbans and attire, flowing beards and the fact that they openly carry their Kirpans [ceremonial daggers carried by Sikhs]

Bars of Mumbai

The Maharashtra government prudently, legalised all forms of spirits and effectively dealt with the problem of illicit liquor; a cause of death and blindness in many states of India. Bars sprang up everywhere, ranging from the Scotch and Wine serving ones to the Quarter bars, to country liquor bars. The former and the latter are the only bars that serve real spirits. The quarter bars serve something called Indian Made Foreign Liquor, which practically translates to distasteful industrially produced spirit that is coloured and flavoured as whisky, rum, gin, brandy and vodka.

Auto Rickshaws

These three wheeled wonders of transport were allowed to ply in Suburban Mumbai sometime in the 70s. These perilous vehicles that are prone to overturning while making 180 degree turns, are now the most used form of public transport, owing to the ease with which they dodge traffic, people and animals. They are allowed to carry three passengers, but it is not uncommon to see a fourth person half seated next to the driver. At stations, they work on a sharing system.

Uncle

When one addresses a man in India as 'Uncle', it implies no relation. It is simply a substitution for the English 'Sir'

Vashi Creek

This creek is what separates main Mumbai from Navi Mumbai [New Mumbai], a mini city created on the mainland, in order to decongest the metropolis. There are three bridges that run over the creek. Two are motor able [one of them occasionally] and one serves the trains.

Jali

This term can denote a net or perforated screen. The beautifully carved Jalis in the palaces of Rajasthan are famous. But the term is also used for humble metal mesh partitions as well.

Smoking in public

In 2003, the Indian Government banned smoking in public spaces and this is largely followed by the citizens. One can be fined or admonished by policemen and marshals if one decided to light up.

Saree and Salwar Kameez

For a large part of India, the traditional dress for women is the Saree, which is an expertly draped unstitched cloth varying from 4.5 to 9 meters in length adorned with beautiful patterns. The modern day women have ditched this for a Salwar Kameez, which is a tunic of varying lengths worn over a pair of leggings and a long scarf [dupatta] that covers the bosom.

Hijra

The term used to refer to transgender in much of India. They are largely shunned by regular society. While some have managed to assimilate, many are forced to survive on alms, handed out by people who view them with a sense of vexation and discomfort.

Chewing gum

Chewing gum has been available in India always. However, for some reason this has not really become very popular, especially amongst the poorer sections. This is possibly because the poor saw little sense in spending money on something to chew that could not be eaten and something that offered no high either [like tobacco].

Sutradhaar : **The Storyteller,**

was born in Calcutta to Debrani and Mihir Lal Mitra,
grew up in Bombay, studied architecture at c e p t ,
Ahmedabad, worked in the Himalayan Kingdom of
Bhutan and now, a driver on the roads of Mumbai

he would love to hear
from you on
hulktoks@gmail.com

Made in the USA
Las Vegas, NV
28 August 2021